Wayne was glad Erin sat beside him in the truck.

He was glad they shared these moments. He didn't feel like he had to pretend with her.

It was overwhelming to feel so at ease with someone. To realize that maybe...opening up could be easier than he had ever imagined.

But at the same time fear breathed through his heart. What was he doing opening up to someone who would vanish from his life again? Someone who wasn't even here by choice? She had landed here because of events outside of her control. She had been forced to settle in Heartmont for the time being. She was caught up in so much turmoil.

The situation with her ex, with her parents and her sister... She probably couldn't think straight. He had to ensure he didn't make it harder for her by showing her any of his feelings. By adding to the complications because...he was falling for her...

Dear Reader,

Thank you so much for picking up the latest book in my Heroes of the Rockies series! If you read the first book, *Winning Over the Rancher*, you may remember the hero's best friend, Wayne. I knew from the start he needed his own story, but I went through a lot of scenarios to decide who was the right woman for him and how they would meet. Somehow it just never seemed to come together, until I decided on the storyline that we have here in *The Rancher and the City Girl*. Wayne showed me that he had a lot of depth and I so wanted him to get his happily-ever-after.

Also, the town of Heartmont is celebrating its 150th anniversary with a grand feast. It seemed fitting to celebrate this safe haven, where my characters always find a place to belong. It's no different for Erin, who lands there almost by chance, having run away from her own wedding. But sometimes, looking back, you realize that things happen for a reason and that hurt and heartache can suddenly, when you least expect it, change to joy and happiness. I hope that Erin and Wayne's story lifts your spirit and encourages you to also keep hoping because new beginnings can be right around the corner.

Warmest wishes,

Viv

THE RANCHER AND THE CITY GIRL

VIV ROYCE

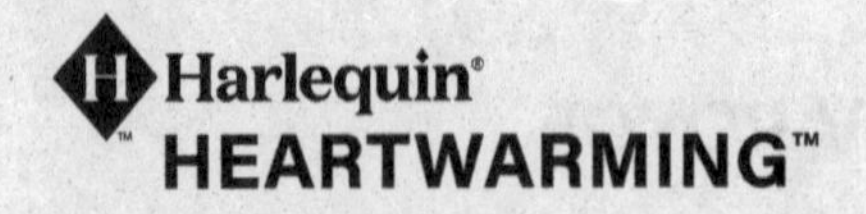

Recycling programs for this product may not exist in your area.

ISBN-13: 978-1-335-46013-4

The Rancher and the City Girl

For questions and comments about the quality of this book, please contact us at CustomerService@Harlequin.com.

TM and ® are trademarks of Harlequin Enterprises ULC.

Harlequin Enterprises ULC
22 Adelaide St. West, 41st Floor
Toronto, Ontario M5H 4E3, Canada
www.Harlequin.com

Printed in U.S.A.

Viv Royce writes uplifting feel-good stories set in tight-knit communities where people fend for each other and love saves the day. If she can fit in lots of delicious food and cute pets, all the better. When she's not plotting the next scene, she can be found crafting, playing board games and trying new ice cream.

Books by Viv Royce

Harlequin Heartwarming

Heroes of the Rockies

Winning Over the Rancher
The Rancher Resolution
A Dad for the Twins

Visit the Author Profile page at Harlequin.com.

Acknowledgments

As always, thanks to all authors (especially Harlequin authors), editors and agents who share online about the writing and publishing process.

Special mention goes to my amazing agent, Jill Marsal, my wonderful editor, Adrienne Macintosh, whose feedback is always spot-on, and to the rest of the dedicated team at Harlequin Heartwarming, especially the cover design team for the evocative cover.

CHAPTER ONE

EVER SINCE SHE had been a little girl, Erin Lakewood had a clear vision of her perfect wedding day. The beautiful white dress, fairy-tale-like with a huge skirt, a long lace train and an embroidered veil the groom would tenderly lift to kiss her. The venue would be grand and romantic, an old country estate with turrets and fireplaces in all the rooms. Her entire family would be there, Mom looking at her with tears of joy in her eyes. Dad would lead her down the aisle to hand her to the groom. He'd wink at her to calm her nerves and assure her he'd always be there for her, even after she had married and started her own family. They had always been so close.

Her older sister Livia would be the perfect wedding organizer, who would make sure everything went down without a glitch. And having always loved flowers and turning them into stunning bouquets for all occasions, Erin would make the best creation ever for that very special day. She'd hold the tender blooms in her hands as she walked down the aisle to her betrothed, surrounded by the people she loved and trusted most in life.

But this morning, having woken up early, even without the need of an alarm clock, she had lain on her back in bed, staring up at the ceiling, feeling like she was, in fact, all alone. Mom and Dad and Livia were not here. They were at home or maybe on the road, traveling for work in their family business, the Lakewood real estate empire. They didn't have an inkling that today was the day. The day their little girl and sis grew up. Married. Took another's name. She hadn't invited them.

Pain slashed through her at the idea and she closed her eyes a moment. How could she have betrayed her family in such an atrocious manner? Locking them out of her life as if they meant nothing to her? There was the occasional phone conversation where they talked about small stuff and carefully avoided the big items. Because over time they had grown apart, separated by the many arguments about her choices.

First there had been the decision not to stay with the family company but instead work on a cruise ship decorating the rooms with flowers and surprising the guests who celebrated birthdays or anniversaries onboard. It satisfied Erin's need for creativity but her parents thought it was a waste of her talents and she should have remained with them, helping to present the luxury properties to their well-to-do clients in the best possible light. Her decision to go against their wishes, for the first time in her life, had chipped the perfect veneer of their relationship and left her feeling abandoned. They rarely asked how her life on the cruise ship was or what cities she had visited. As if they hoped that by not showing any interest in her current life, they could make her regret her choice and return to them. If they thought that, they didn't understand her at all. After every phone call where it was all about them and they didn't even ask how she was doing, beyond an opening "How are you?"

"Oh, fine," she felt more detached from them and more determined to make her own life work out with or without their approval.

And then Hutch had come into her life and swept her off her feet. Again, her family had not agreed with her choice. Had actually been vehemently opposed, even accusing him of being a player who used his work on the cruise ship to hit on women, or a gold digger, merely after her family's money. They hadn't wanted her to date him, let alone marry him. So when Hutch had popped the question, presenting her with a gorgeous ring with a pink stone in it, she had accepted with a happy heart and at the same time a tidal wave of dread at having to tell her family about it. She didn't want to hear their reasons why it would never work out with Hutch and her. Not when she had already decided she wanted to be with him for the rest of her life.

Then Hutch had said they didn't need to tell them at all. That it was their decision and that people often married without their family present. That it was their day, their moment to celebrate their love.

"It's just better that way, baby," Hutch had told her, kissing her softly on the temple.

It had seemed he was right. No arguments on their happy day, no silent reproaches in her parents' eyes as they watched how their daughter promised to share her life with the man they had never wanted for her.

"I can't help it that they never liked me," Hutch had said in a hurt tone. "I tried hard enough to fit into your posh family. But they always made me feel like I wasn't good enough. Not in your league. They're upper-class and look down on a working man like me. Had I been a hotshot lawyer or architect, they would have liked me well enough."

Erin had cringed at this assessment. Even though her parents had been cold to Hutch, his conviction that it was about money or status was all wrong. Her family wasn't snobby at all. They interacted with people from all walks of life. Just because they had lots of money and often dealt with the rich and famous in their business, that didn't mean that they isolated themselves. Besides, they also worked hard to earn their living. They had experienced lean years before achieving the success they now had with Lakewood Real Estate. Hutch acted like it had all come easy to them, and maybe they didn't even really deserve it.

But Hutch was right that her family didn't approve of him. Did it even matter what the exact reason was? Whether they had her best interests at heart or were only seeing what they wanted to see? Facts were that they didn't like him and they hoped for the relationship to end.

It had been such a letdown as she had so wanted her family to love the man she had fallen for. She still couldn't believe that he had also fallen for her. Hutch who was so sporty and strong, funny and popular. The most wanted bachelor in their group of cruise ship attendants using their leave to go on a skiing holiday in the Rocky Mountains. She had seen him and felt the attraction like a jolt of electricity. But she had known that a girl like her, pretty average, could never have him. Others would, while she watched. It had always been like that from high school through college and beyond.

Strangely enough, Hutch had singled her out and been attentive, kind, funny. He had taught her how to ski better and they had built a snow fort and ambushed the others from behind its frozen walls. It had been perfect. Especially when he had leaned over and brushed the snow off her face and then kissed her. Finally someone had chosen her and she intended to fully enjoy that wonderful feeling. Even if she had to oppose her parents and Livia. She had her own life now. She should follow her heart.

And here they were, back in the Rockies, where it had all started. Hutch had said it was fitting. His mother had chosen the venue, telling Erin she had always wanted to stay at this resort. Erin didn't see the attraction. It was a modern building, nice enough if you cared for red brick and too many windows, but it had no turrets and no real old fireplaces. Just ones with fake electric flames.

Like everything about my relationship with Hutch is fake.

Erin cringed at the thought whispering through her mind like a treacherous wind stirring up the calm of a lake. She wanted to enjoy this day to the full, not have it spoiled by second-guessing. She was going to marry Hutch. In three more hours they'd be man and wife. Nothing could prevent that.

Not even Livia arriving in a fury to tell her she couldn't go on with the ceremony. If she had somehow found out… She'd be so mad.

And so hurt.

Her heart sank at the idea. She had never meant to cause Livia any pain. Or their parents. When they had talked on the phone a few days ago, she had still toyed with the idea of telling them anyway. Because it had felt so strange to leave them totally in the dark. But fear of their response and the day being ruined had held her back. She just had to be strong and make the choices that were right for her, for her future. She wanted Hutch, needed Hutch. More than oxygen. He told her she was pretty, that he couldn't live without her. And she wanted to believe him. She had given up everything for him, had quit her job on the cruise ship. After their honeymoon she would start working at a flower shop.

Hutch had arranged the job for her, at a shop on a block close to the office building where he had started an investment business with a college buddy. Hutch had said they'd definitely need two incomes to have weekends away. He had said he wanted only the best for her. But for her it need not all be big and fancy. They'd have fun close to their apartment. There were plenty of museums and cinemas, restaurants and cute little delis to pick up food and then have a picnic in the park. The city was alive around the clock, inviting them to so many fun activities from an underground escape room in an old metro station to breathtaking views from a rooftop tearoom. The world would lie at their feet. They could do anything, together.

She stared into the mirror, into the wide blue eyes looking back at her. There were rumors Hutch hadn't quit his job on the cruise ship, but had been fired. For unacceptable behavior with female passengers. He had denied it. Had said it was just vicious lies. That he had been fired to protect another officer who was related to the captain. She had believed him.

She had to believe the man who was going

to be her husband. Or their marriage would never work.

Her hands slowly smoothed the fabric of her wedding dress. She had wanted to try it on one more time before the ceremony. There was no need to smooth it really as it was super tight. There was no big skirt and no long train and no veil even. Hutch had told her he hated that, it was old-fashioned and stiff. He wanted something cocktail dress-like. "Imagine you're going to the Oscars, baby. You need a bit more star quality."

The dress was pretty enough. But it wasn't her. It wasn't her dream. She was playing out someone else's scenario. But this wasn't a movie. This was her life. She could only do this once. She wanted to do it right.

She stared into her reflection's petrified gaze. *It's too late for that. You didn't speak up earlier and now...you just have to live with it.*

The dress, the venue. At least everyone else liked it. Hutch and his parents, his brothers, his grandparents, his cousins, his friends. All of his family and acquaintances who had traveled here to be part of Hutch's and her big day. Over sixty people. At her expense. *After all,* Hutch had said, *you have some money in the bank, baby, savings. I just put everything I had into my new business with Arthur. We so deserve this shot, you know.*

He did and she wanted him to succeed. She didn't really begrudge him the expenses paid from her pocket for this special day.

But all the guests belonged to his party and…almost none belonged to hers. She had invited a few cruise ship colleagues as bridesmaids but even that felt funny. When they had sipped cocktails last night and she had looked at their faces, they might as well have been total strangers. They had acted like they hardly knew her. No one had asked how she felt, had put an arm around her. They had just made shallow jokes.

It was all fake. She ached to run away. But she had to go through with it. Live out the day.

And then? a voice questioned. *Then you are married to him. Stuck with him and his overbearing mother, the friends who are constantly sponging off him. Didn't you overhear last night how his cousin wanted to borrow money?*

She closed her eyes and took a deep breath. It was perfectly normal not to like everyone you met. And maybe under the pressure she was exaggerating their vices. She just had to get to know them better.

Still, she wished she had put her foot down

about the dress. She could compromise on the venue maybe, but the dress… This was so not her style. And she did want a veil. Could she ask someone from the hotel to get her a veil? If need be, make one from a lacy curtain?

But she cringed as she imagined her soon-to-be mother-in-law seeing Erin with some "old and ugly headpiece" as she would no doubt call it. No. It was too late. This was it. The veil had just been a childhood fantasy. It didn't matter as long as she married the man she loved. And she did love Hutch.

She reached up to lift her shoulder-length hair and shape it into a casual bun at the back of her head. The hairdresser would be here in half an hour. She had brought a diamond-encrusted comb, a gift from her grandmother, for this special day.

Erin looked for it on the dressing table but it wasn't there. She frowned. Had she shown it to her bridesmaid Jenn the other day? Of course. It had to be in her room.

Already at the door leading into the corridor, Erin hesitated. What if she happened to run into Hutch? He was staying in a separate wing with his friends, but he might be up and about, to ease his nerves or something. He shouldn't see her in her wedding dress. It would spoil the surprise.

She picked up a light red raincoat and slipped it on over the dress. That was better.

She opened the door and peeked out. No one in sight. She went to Jenn's bedroom door and knocked softly. No need to wake anyone else up. No reply.

She tried the door. *Open.*

She peeked in. The bed had been slept in but Jenn was gone.

Erin grinned. Of course. Jenn always started her day off with a glass of lukewarm water and lemon juice. Was great for the skin, she claimed. She had to be in the kitchen downstairs. Erin tiptoed down the stairs, careful not to create any creaking noises. Despite her raincoat cover she didn't want to be seen by anyone. A breach of tradition.

She was close to the archway leading into the kitchen when she heard the sound. Suppressed laughter. Was Jenn not alone in there? Had she better go back up? But she did want to know where the comb was. It was valuable.

She stepped forward and got a full view of the kitchen counter. There was a glass of water on it. Beside it, Jenn sat on the counter her back to Erin, in her tight sport pants and top with

BABE emblazoned on the back. Strong male hands rested just below the word. The guy had his head bent down to hers, kissing her.

Erin wanted to step away. She had obviously caught her colleague at an awkward moment. That one cousin of Hutch's had been making eyes at her over dinner last night so maybe…

But the cousin was blond. This guy had dark hair and…

As he raised his head, Erin got a clear look at his face.

She blinked. A hot sensation grabbed her chest, pushing blood into her cheeks. Her feet seemed to sink through the floorboards and then move back up, her gut clenching.

Hutch.

It was Hutch kissing Jenn.

Her groom and one of her bridesmaids. Three hours before the wedding.

"I still think we're taking too much of a risk," Jenn said as she ran her hand across Hutch's chest.

"I love risks." His voice was husky. "Look, Erin is still in bed or turning about in front of the mirror like some peacock. I bet you I will hate the dress she chose. She once showed me in a magazine what she wanted. Big skirt, train, miles of lace. Ugh."

"I think your mother took care of that." Jenn laughed. "She drilled your bride to perfection. The girl hasn't got a chance in the world."

If it had been a stranger there with Hutch, a woman she knew only vaguely, or the receptionist from the resort, it would have been hurtful to see them together and hear them laugh at her. But this was one of her colleagues. Someone she had considered to be a friend. Someone she could count on, not someone who stabbed her in the back.

She swallowed hard. She wanted to be the person who rushed in and smacked them both and told them that they had to leave. That Hutch had to pay for the entire wedding no matter if it broke his fledgling business. He had brought her here, pretending he wanted to marry her, while…

He loved someone else?

No.

He didn't love Jenn either. She was just a thrill to him, something new. Something forbidden. That was the way he was.

She should have known it after his dismissal. She had reassured herself, clinging to his story that it was all lies, wrongful accusations by someone higher up, covered by the captain's authority. She had wanted to believe it, to keep her world together.

But she should have accepted her losses then. Accepted the awful truth that Hutch was a player. That he had only chosen her to marry because she was meek and gullible and didn't want to hear a bad word about him. Because he could wrap her around his finger time and time again. No matter what others said, she always believed him.

She had made it so easy for him to take advantage of her.

She should have realized that before it was too late.

Because it is too late now.

Right?

She stepped back and turned around, so grateful that they had been too preoccupied to see her. She walked away without making a sound. Inside she was screaming but she never made a peep. She went up the stairs and into her room, locked the door and walked to the bed. She sank on the edge of it and sat staring into the distance.

She could act like she hadn't seen them. Pretend she didn't know. She could go into marriage with an unfaithful man, knowing he would be unfaithful over and over. Lots of women encountered that problem. She was certainly not alone.

Did she really want to cancel the wedding? Face the shame and embarrassment? Especially as the reason became known?

But did anyone have to find out? Could she not pretend that she had gotten cold feet? That she had changed her mind? That being here with all of his family had shown her what she was getting into? Could she not…leave in dignity?

Dignity?!

She almost laughed. Her hands grabbed the duvet and crinkled it so hard the fabric almost tore. There was nothing left of her dignity. Hutch had lied to her about everything. About loving her, wanting the best for her. He was a selfish monster who was willing to get married at her expense while he was betraying her. She should have listened to her parents, to Livia. They had warned her that Hutch was unreliable. But she had ignored them, even cut them out of the equation by not inviting them to the wedding.She would love to crawl under the bed and never show herself again.

She had made herself into the biggest fool alive.

She got up and with mechanical movements

gathered her things. Her purse, phone, jewelry from the little safe hidden in the closet. There she found the comb she had been looking for. If she had realized earlier where it was, she would have stayed in her room and never have discovered the betrayal.

But she had.

New tears filled her eyes and she just wanted to run. She could send for the rest of her luggage later. If she left now she might have a chance to escape unseen.

She ran to the door and unlocked it, took a deep breath. She opened it a crack and peered out. *Nothing. Good.*

She raced down the stairs and turned away from the kitchen area, leaving via the French doors in the living room area. Across the terrace. Down the path to the main building.

Staff was busy preparing the outside seating area. Chairs with white bows on them and flower arrangements on the tables. Each little detail broke another piece off her heart. She hadn't wanted to marry here or with these people present, but at least she had believed she was marrying for love. Now she had lost everything, every bit of hope, every bit of...confidence that she could make the right decisions. She couldn't. She was a failure. An utter hopeless failure.

Wiping at the tears leaking down her face, she rounded the building to the front, just as a tall man with a cowboy hat, checkered shirt and dark jeans was about to get into his pickup truck. He waved at the waiter who held a crate with something deep red. Cherries?

"Wait!" She ran to the man with the cowboy hat. "Can you give me a ride? I will pay you generously. I need to leave here in a real hurry."

He looked her over. His gaze lingered on the white dress underneath the raincoat. Paired with sneakers it was a strange combination. "Getting married, are you?"

"Yes. I could try and call a cab but we are pretty remote so it would take time for it to get here. Too much time." She forced a smile. She had to let him believe she had to get to the wedding location quickly. She'd explain on the road.

"I see. Congratulations on your wedding. Get in then." He glanced at her face, a look of concern crossing his features. "Nervous? Looks like you've been crying."

"I'm fine." She got into the passenger seat and buckled up. The seat belt closed around her like a safety line anchoring her to the choice she had made. Whatever happened next she was not marrying Hutch. She was not *ever* marrying him.

The cowboy climbed in and looked at her. "Where to then?"

Her mind stopped a moment. She didn't know. Everything she had been living for was right here. Where to now?

Think! Think of something.

On the way to the resort she had seen a sign from the car. Heartmont. It had rung a bell because a former colleague of hers, April Williams, lived there. At a ranch hotel, with the man she had married.

April had found true love, of course. Other people weren't duped like she had been.

New tears rose in her eyes. With a trembling voice she said, "I need to go to Heartmont."

"Okay." He nodded. "That's where I live so I know it well." And he hit the gas, removing her from the place she never wanted to lay eyes on again.

CHAPTER TWO

WAYNE DIDN'T KNOW what to say. A sensation that was totally new to him. He usually had a smart remark for every situation. But this woman was obviously as tight as a string on a fiddle. And she had been crying. He could still see the telltale redness around her eyes. She was getting married and she was crying. That wasn't good.

Or was it? Didn't women cry tears of happiness sometimes? Maybe she was just emotional because it was the big day at last. Having prepared for it for weeks. Months probably. Weddings were a big deal. Not that he had any experience with it. He had carefully avoided getting attached to anyone. He didn't have relationships. He only dated every now and then.

If he had to.

If he had the time for it.

Which he rarely had with his ranch and all of his local obligations. Especially now that his best buddy Cade spent more time at his orchard ranch because his wife was pregnant. Wayne knew how Cade and his wife Lily had been looking forward to having a baby. Both Cade and Lily were totally besotted with Cade's sister Gina's kids: the vivacious twins Stacey and Ann and baby boy Barry. Well, everybody kept calling him the baby of the family but he was turning two already later this year. It was great that his mom had found love recently with a ranger and would be moving away from the ranch soon to have her own home again. But Cade had confided in Wayne that he would really miss those kids. So Lily and he were over the moon to start their own family.

Wayne understood because he saw how happy they were. But he didn't need that kind of thing himself. He was perfectly content when he came home and could kick off his boots in the hallway and drop his jacket over a chair in the kitchen and not have anyone tell him to pick up his things. There was no one to question him about his lack of ambition in choosing to be a small-town rancher while he could have been a high-flying lawyer if only he had tried harder. No one to object to shoving a pizza in the oven for the third night in a row because there were healthier dinner choices. Pizza was healthy. Kind of.

He suppressed a smile and then quickly checked himself, glancing at the passenger beside him. It wasn't nice laughing when she was so…sad. That was the right word for it. She was sad. He saw it in her blue eyes that stared ahead without seeing the road. She looked like she was about to cry again.

He cleared his throat uncomfortably. "Uh, where in Heartmont can I drop you? Are you getting married at the community center? Or the church maybe?"

She swallowed hard. The sound touched him in an unexpected way. Her vulnerability made him want to stop the truck and reach out to put his hand on her arm. To tell her it would be okay again, somehow. But he didn't know what she was thinking. She might just be nervous. Worried not everything would go down without a glitch. Women liked things to be perfect. Another reason why he didn't have a girlfriend. Because his life was far from perfect. He himself was far from perfect.

He could still hear his father tell him: *look, Wayne, you need to do better. This isn't good enough. You need to become more than we all have ever been. You need to rise above it.*

He clenched the wheel. His father had pinned a lot of hopes and expectations on him. That he could make captain of the football team, that he could get a scholarship. That he could go to college and then university and become a lawyer maybe. Someone who would make the family proud. But he had been okay at football but not good enough for a scholarship. He had never liked studying from books and had gone from high school straight into jobs earning money to buy land and start his own ranch. That was what he had wanted to do. Be a rancher, not a lawyer in the city who sat in an office all day long. He had let Dad down. He had let Mom down. Not that he had even known his mother. She had died when he had been but a little boy. But Dad had told him often enough what Mom had wanted for him. Something better than what they had.

There had always been this feeling that it had to be something that was out of reach. That you could never be happy with what you had, with where you were. Wayne had become tired of it. He had told himself: when I grow up, I want to have a place that I love, do work that I love and then be glad that I have it. I don't want to spend my life chasing something I will never achieve.

But he had let his family down. He knew that in the back of his head. It was a thing at the edges of his existence always ready to close in again like sudden morning fog.

He shook himself to return to the present. He had asked her a question. Had she responded? "Sorry," he said, "I was distracted a moment."

She took a deep breath. "I uh…need to get to a hotel. That is, it is a ranch hotel. I don't know the exact address, but if you live in Heartmont, you probably know it. It's run by a man named Matt. He is married to April."

"Matt Carpenter. Sure, I know him and April. April is the younger sister of my best buddy Cade Williams. We used to be the terror of our local school. Always pulling pranks on everybody."

He caught a twitch at the corners of her mouth as if she had to smile involuntarily. Encouraged, he continued, "We used to have a teacher in third grade who used a wooden stick to point out things on the blackboard. One time we snuck into the classroom and made a cut in the stick so that when she swung it toward the blackboard, it broke in halves. One part clattered to the floor. The bewildered look on her face was priceless. Everybody laughed so she never knew who actually did it." He grinned at the memory. "I guess it was all pretty innocent. We were bored with school and we thought up ways to make it all a little more exciting. Or at least amusing." He glanced at her again. "Did you like school?"

ERIN BLINKED AT the question. Her head was a turmoil of questions. She could about scream at the bad hand life had dealt her with this miserable situation she was stuck in and he asked whether she had liked school?

She faltered, "Uhm, yeah, I guess so. I was pretty good at most subjects and..." She had liked being a straight A student. To feel that the teachers admired her effort and results. She had wanted to do well to please her parents.

She had probably been the girl in his class that he hated for being so perfect. At least it was her experience that people who didn't like learning so much often disliked the top students, thinking they were somehow arrogant.

"What was your favorite subject?" he asked.

"History," she replied in a heartbeat. "I loved to hear about earlier times, how people lived, the choices they made and how little things impacted entire peoples in a major way. I found it all fascinating." After a moment's thought she added, "A little scary too."

"Scary? You mean the tales of war and all, bloodshed?" he queried.

"No. The idea that choices we make have such enormous consequences." Like the choice to marry the wrong man? She swallowed hard.

He nodded as he looked at the road ahead. "That's life. Can't change a thing about it."

"But you can think about it. Hope to do better. You don't want to let people down. Especially people who are important to you." She clenched her hands together.

A frown furrowed his brow a moment as if her remark made him pause, but he didn't comment. "So you are getting married at the ranch hotel?" he asked. "It is a very nice venue. Not big but it has an authentic feel about it. You must love horses. I also have a few."

"That's nice." She said it automatically, her head spinning with the question of what on earth she was doing. She had run away from her own wedding. They would discover she was gone. They would look for her and not find her. She should have left them a note to say she was okay. Now there would be total chaos, a search for her around the property. Or would someone start by trying to call her?

As if on cue, her phone rang. The sound coming from her purse drove a shock through her body. She looked out of the side window at the trees as if searching for a way to escape. A path to run down and never come back. But she had to face this sometime.

"Is that your phone ringing?" the driver asked. He shot her an inquisitive look from his deep brown eyes. There was a quiet concern in them as if he sensed her tension.

"Uh, yes, I better answer it." She struggled to get it out of the purse. It almost slid from her sweaty palms and dropped between her feet. He had to think she was the clumsiest person on earth. Hutch had often said she was clumsy. Clumsy but cute. She had taken it as a compliment. She had accepted everything he said and did rather than risk losing him.

Tears burned in her eyes as she picked up the phone. "Hello?"

"Jenn here. Where are you? Everybody is looking for you." Her colleague's voice sounded cheerful. Nothing gave away that she had betrayed Erin. That she had kissed her groom and had said nasty things about Erin. No, she sounded perfectly normal. "The wedding is about to start. We do need a bride."

At those last words something inside Erin snapped. "Do you?" she asked, her voice trembling with anger. "Why, may I ask? Why do you need a bride? To have someone gullible enough to marry Hutch while he is playing around with the bridesmaid?"

There was a shocked silence on the other end of the line. Jenn took a deep breath. It rustled across the connection. "You saw us?"

"I saw enough to draw my own conclusions."

"Erin, don't. Hutch does love you. He doesn't care one thing for me. I don't care for him. It's just a fling. We didn't mean to hurt anyone. Let alone ruin the wedding. Come on inside. I can explain everything to you."

Jenn apparently thought she had gone outside and was walking about, in a daze after her discovery. "I don't want to hear any explanations. From you or Hutch. I understand it all."

"Erin, please." Jenn sounded irritated more than sorry. "You are behaving like a baby. Or like someone who has never been around. On the ship we all had affairs. With fellow staff, with passengers. It happens. You are away from home in a happy holiday mood, you see someone you like and… Well, it is not something to be proud of I guess, but it's only human. You have to think about the consequences if you don't come back now. Hutch's entire family is here."

"Yes." *His is, mine is not. Because I was silly*

enough to choose his side. I sacrificed it all for him and he wasn't worth it. She clenched the phone. "You tell them what happened. You know, right?"

"Erin, don't act like a toddler whose candy was taken. Hutch is a grown man. He has been with women before. Consider this his last taste of freedom."

"Before he gets all locked up in marriage. If that is how he feels, he had better stay a bachelor. Why marry at all?" *Unless it is for money. My money.* Erin closed her eyes a moment. Her parents had been right. Livia too. She had been taken advantage of. And she had let it happen. Because she had wanted to be loved. Not for her assets but for herself.

"Wait a sec," Jenn said. "Here is Hutch."

Erin wanted to put the phone down before she could hear his voice, but it was too late already. There it was, that warm brown sugar voice purring at her. "Hey babe, what's the matter? Where are you? We are all waiting for you. I want to see you in your dress. I heard from Mom it is spectacular."

"She loves it, yes," Erin said in a low voice.

"Babe, come on over now. Everything is alright. The thing you saw with Jenn and me... Just a little goodbye kiss. Nothing special. I love you. I need you. You know that. I have always needed you."

Tears burned in her eyes as she listened to the lies she had often enough believed. Had wanted to believe, to hang on to the dream of the wedding and having her own place and…

She blinked and hot tears coursed down her cheeks. She tried to keep herself from falling apart completely. He kept saying he loved her after what he had done. How could he?

"Are you okay?"

The voice reached her as if from afar. She realized she was in a truck with a stranger who had picked her up and was now driving her to Heartmont. She felt so ashamed of her tears she did not dare look at him. She just nodded vaguely and said into the phone, "I am not coming back. I am not going to marry you. Cancel that party. Tell your family. You ruined it all. You should be the one to tell them." She disconnected without even saying goodbye.

The phone rang again, but she didn't answer. When it kept ringing she turned it off with an angry gesture. Tears kept rolling down her face and she felt totally humiliated. He expected her to just marry him even though she knew he had been unfaithful. But then as Jenn had put it, everyone was, right?

The driver asked again, "Are you alright?" Before she could say anything, he added, "That's a weird question, because I can see you are not alright. And I overheard enough of the conversation to get why. But I uh… I guess I should say something encouraging, but I don't really know what to say."

"That makes two of us. I don't know what to say either. I made you believe I was getting married while I was really running away from my wedding."

"At the resort?" he asked and she nodded.

"His family chose it. I never liked it. I never liked any of it. Still, I went along with it because…" She couldn't go on and hid her face in her hands.

WAYNE CLENCHED THE WHEEL. This was the moment to say all kinds of helpful things. But his head was empty. Except for one question. What kind of man hurt a woman in such a manner? What kind of man had driven this sweet girl into flight? She looked so helpless sitting beside him in that raincoat over her wedding dress, crying. He wanted to do something to stop her from feeling miserable but he knew it was impossible. She should have been happy today. She should have felt safe in the arms of the man who had promised to take care of her. But everything had gone wrong. At least she had had the guts to walk away from it all, to not go through with the wedding under pressure because all of the guests were there. She had made a choice to go against the grain, like he had once done. But he knew there was a price to pay for that. She probably didn't fully get yet how hard this would be because people would blame her for her decision. While none of it was her fault.

"I am sorry," he said, catching the emotion in his own voice. "I am really really sorry. You don't deserve this. I mean, I'm sure you prepared for it with the best intentions and you wanted to love him and be loyal to him and then..."

"I guess I should have known," she said in a strained voice. "All the signs were there. I just didn't want to see them. I was so happy and I wanted to keep going."

"There is no harm in that."

"No harm?" She looked at him with flashing eyes. "I lied to myself."

"I mean, there is no harm in wanting to be happy. Most people want that, right? And if he lied to you, and you believed him, how is that your fault?"

"Because I shouldn't have been so naive. So willing to believe every lie he told me just because I loved him." She clenched her hands into fists. "I was an easy victim. He must be laughing his head off now."

"I don't think so. I think he is pretty worried about what he has to tell his family. They are all there waiting for a wedding that won't take place because you made a decision to protect yourself." As Wayne said it, a sort of relief breathed through him. It was not taking place. She was not getting married to that jerk who had betrayed her. She had found out in time. She was safe now. He would make sure of that.

"Listen," he said. "I'll drive you to the ranch hotel and you can talk to April. I'm sure you will feel better then. And you simply keep your phone turned off so they can't find you."

"I feel so silly dressed like this," she said, gesturing at her outfit. "It is not even the dress I wanted."

He wanted to ask what dress she had wanted but it would be painful to discuss that on this unhappy day. He cleared his throat and said, "Well, I can drive you to a clothes store, I guess, but it would be a bit weird for you to walk in there dressed like this. In a small town people gossip easily and..."

"Please don't take me anywhere where people can see me," she said shrinking back in her seat. "I don't want to become the talk of the town."

"The ranch hotel is best then," he said. "You can get out of the car and go straight inside. The door is always open even if April isn't there. The reception will be open. That will be Matt's dad sitting there or a volunteer. But don't worry, they will be discreet once they hear you are a friend of April's."

She sighed. "The term friend doesn't really apply, I guess. I know April only vaguely. We worked on the same cruise ship for a while. It's not like we are close friends and I can just drop in uninvited."

"You can always drop in uninvited at their place. So you are a cruise ship attendant. How nice."

She didn't engage. She sat huddled like a hurt little bird staring at her phone on her lap. "Don't you turn it back on," he said and she looked up at him, flushing as if she was caught red-handed.

"I have never before—" her voice cracked "—left people in a mess. A jam, whatever you want to call it. I am always the one solving problems, not creating them."

"He can solve this one on his own. Trust me." Wayne smiled at her, trying to coax a response out of her troubled eyes. "He had this coming."

"I just wish I had found out earlier. Not on this very day. There are almost sixty guests." She sounded close to panic now. "How can I simply run and leave them all sitting there?"

"I guess your family will be worried where you are," he agreed reluctantly. "Maybe you should call them to explain before they hear it from the disgruntled groom."

"They are not there. They couldn't attend. They're busy with their business." She said it quickly, without looking at him.

He sensed there was something more behind this. Had they not agreed with her choice of a partner? Had they distrusted him? With good reason it appeared. That had to be extra hard on her.

She pushed the phone back in her purse and sighed. The sound trembled on the air. "I just don't understand why this had to happen to me. I am always so careful. I never take chances, you know. I avoid risks." She scoffed. "Now I feel like I've lost all my brownie points."

"There is an advantage."

"Huh?" She cast him a bewildered look.

"Once you lose all your brownie points, there is nothing left to cling to and preserve with all your might. You are free to do what you want, be who you are."

ERIN BLINKED. REALLY? As her entire life crumbled around her, he threw some platitudes at her. About being the person you wanted to be. Like that was even possible. There were always expectations hanging over your head. Other people's, your own.

She played with the cuff of her raincoat. She could only hope the ranch hotel wouldn't be much further away. She needed to get out of this truck. It seemed the space was getting smaller by the minute.

"By the way," he said, "my name is Wayne. Wayne Irvine."

"Erin Lakewood," she replied automatically. As she said it, she cringed, wishing she had left her last name out. To her mind the name Lakewood could easily link her to her parents' successful real estate empire, and her situation right now was so embarrassing it shouldn't in any way involve them. It felt like it would somehow taint them, and their relationship with her would deteriorate even further.

"Nice to meet you," he said. "How do you like the Rocky Mountains?"

Erin blinked a moment. "Actually, I hate them. This is where I met Hutch. And this is where that lousy traitor two-timed me."

"I see. But he is not a local, is he?"

"No. Why do you ask"

"Then we still have a chance to show you that we are good folks living here. That it was just a coincidence that you met this guy here."

Erin nodded slowly. Would it ever feel like that? Just a coincidence she had met Hutch and fallen for him? Bad timing? A temporary slip? But at least she had seen the truth in time, had escaped the marriage, was a free woman still.

Maybe someday she would see it that way.

But definitely not today.

CHAPTER THREE

APRIL CARPENTER STOOD in the kitchen of the ranch hotel she ran with her husband Matt Carpenter and his father, and stared hard at the cans on the counter to make a decision. She was in charge of desserts for the night and she couldn't quite decide whether it was going to be canned peaches or pears on her cake. Outside the sound of a car engine resounded. She glanced at her watch. Matt wasn't due back for at least an hour. His father had gone to a friend's ranch to help repair a tractor. He was great with engines. There weren't any new guests arriving today. So who could that be?

She wiped her hands on her apron and went to the window to glance outside. The truck that halted was very familiar. Wayne. What could he want? He probably had something to ask Matt. It would have been better if he had called before dropping in and finding Matt gone. It wasn't that she didn't like seeing Wayne but his arrival was a bit of a distraction with her cake baking in progress and her plans to go visit her sister Gina and the kids afterward. Of course Gina was the better baker of the two of them but baking was her profession so it was also nice to try some goodies once in a while just as a treat.

April blinked as she watched the passenger door of the truck open and a young woman climb out. She looked like a model with her light makeup and hair pulled back in a stylish bun, the raincoat half-open over a stunning wedding dress. Who on earth could that be? How did Wayne know such a woman? In the past he had the reputation of being a bit of a ladies' man because he had dated a lot but never gotten serious with any of the women he went out with. Lately however he was too busy with his ranch, caring for injured horses and picking up Cade's committee work for the town now that Lily was pregnant. April could never quite get a handle on Wayne's ideas when it came to relationships. He usually laughed off any question in that direction. Maybe he just liked to be alone?

April went outside to greet them. As she closed in on the two of them, she seemed to detect something familiar in the woman's features. She also noticed a little redness around her eyes as if she had been crying.

Wayne said, "Hey April, sorry to be dropping in like this, but I picked up Erin on the way back from the mountain resort and I thought I could play taxi. She wants to stay with you for a few days. Have a bit of downtime, for herself."

"Erin, yes, I thought there was something familiar about you. We worked together, didn't we? On the ship. You made all those gorgeous flower arrangements. I remember now. How did you end up out here?" April gave Erin a hug and a kiss on the cheek. "You must excuse how I look, but I was baking. Come on inside. I'd love to show you the hotel. My husband and his father did a great job getting it to where it is now. I love being a part of it. We also have horses. You can see them later. Please come in. You too, Wayne."

Wayne made a dismissive gesture. "I am already late for my next appointment. You two chat. Catch up." He dug a card from his pocket and gave it to Erin. "You call me later. If you need anything. You know."

April stared at the look on Wayne's face as he stepped back. It was rather sheepish as if he was out of his depths here. Was it possible there was a woman who had actually touched Wayne's heart? He was the eternal bachelor, the prank player, the man with a smooth reply to everything. A rogue on the outside, a good guy on the inside. Who was alone too much, she guessed.

Wayne retreated to his vehicle, got in and drove off. He didn't even sound the horn as he usually did.

April looked at Erin again. Wayne had simply made it sound like Erin was here for a short vacation. But people usually didn't take a vacation in their wedding dress. Something was up. But judging by Erin's red eyes it was better not to ask anything now or there might be a flood of tears. She had to involve her in some innocent activity to get her a little more relaxed. "Let's go into the kitchen. I have to keep an eye on the oven. I was just deciding about the topping for my cake. You can help me."

Erin followed her up the steps. "What a nice place," she said. "Really cozy." Her voice was a little unsteady.

April opened the screen door for her and they went inside. Once in the hot kitchen, April said, "Do take off the raincoat. It is so warm in here with the oven on." She went to check on it, peering through the glass panel at her two cake tins. "It smells nice," Erin said.

"Yes, I swirled in some chocolate batter as well. It always looks good when you cut the cake. Sit down and I'll pour you a cup of coffee. It is still pretty fresh."

She busied herself with mugs, the coffeepot, sugar.

Erin had sat down. She stared at her hands on the table. Then she looked at April and said, "You haven't asked me what I am doing here. Or…why I am dressed like this."

April held her gaze. It was hard to see the sadness there. The pain. Something was wrong, she did know that. She said softly, "It's not for me to ask. But for you to tell me when you are ready."

"I don't think I will ever be ready. Ready to say it out loud to someone else. I can't even bear to say it to myself. That it's all over."

April's heart shrank. Erin wasn't a close friend of hers, just someone she had worked with, but when a woman wore a wedding dress and said it was all over, it had to hurt. It was the end of a dream. The destruction of that fantasy of the big day, the white dress, the guests and the cake and the flowers… Everything Erin had dreamt of now ruined.

April sat down opposite her and shoved the coffee mug toward her. "There, drink something. Careful, it's hot."

Erin sipped gratefully. Then she said, "I was here at the resort to get married. I had met this wonderful man… A cruise attendant too, ironically. I don't know if you ever heard of him. Worked with him. Hutch Michaels."

April shook her head. "I can't say I have, but I met so many people in my career."

"It doesn't really matter. It seems like I'm losing myself in pointless details. In the truck Wayne and I even talked about our favorite subjects in school. It was so…random. Still, it was nice. Not to think about reality." A sad smile touched Erin's lips.

April smiled too, thinking of Wayne who was considered a clown but who did have the tact to handle this right. It was a good thing he had found Erin and brought her here. In their close-knit community everyone would rally around her to help out.

Erin said, "Hutch asked me to marry him and then we got into this whirlwind of preparations. The wedding, our apartment. He started a business with a friend and got me a job at a flower shop near the apartment."

"Oh, you two stopped cruising?" April asked.

Erin sighed. "Hutch quit, he said, but rumor had it he was fired. For womanizing with passengers. I didn't want to believe it. But I guess it was true." She sipped her coffee again.

April waited for her to continue.

Erin said, "I wanted to believe in him, you know. In us. In how perfect it had been from the start. How we met, how he fell for me and…it was so romantic, something straight out of a movie. But I guess it was just too good to be true. Fairy tales don't exist. This morning when I needed something and left my room at the resort to go and get it I saw him kissing one of my bridesmaids. They were also talking about me and saying…" Her voice trailed off and she just sat there, head down.

April felt a jolt of anger. How could anyone do this? Betray someone, hurt them, make them feel so small and insignificant?

She reached out and put her hand on Erin's arm. "I am so sorry for you."

Erin nodded slowly. "I ran away. I couldn't stay there. I just ran and…outside a truck was parked. A man was going to leave the resort. I just asked him for a ride. That was Wayne."

"He must have been surprised," April said.

"At first he thought I was getting married

in town. That he had to take me to the venue. He was so nice about it." Erin fussed with her hands. "But then my phone rang. It was Jenn. The bridesmaid who…"

"Did she want to apologize?"

"No. Not at all." Erin seemed to get angry now. "She told me in a commanding tone that I had to come back and marry Hutch. That it was just a fling between them, nothing serious. That he cared for me and still wanted to marry me."

"The nerve! How could she say such things to you?"

"I guess to them this lifestyle is normal? I don't know. She did say something about all of us having affairs while cruising."

April shook her head. "Not all of us."

Erin gave her a watery smile. "Then Hutch came on the line. He said that he still cared and…whatnot. I don't even remember exactly. It was all a blur. But I am not going back."

"Oh, you shouldn't. You can of course stay here. We have a room available."

"I didn't bring much with me." Erin gestured.

April said, "You can borrow some of my clothes. We're about the same size. It will be fine. You don't have to go back."

ERIN HEARD THE words *you don't have to go back* and then something broke inside of her. All she could do was hold her hands to her face and sob. She was normally very calm and collected and this whole situation was super embarrassing. But April didn't say anything. She just came over and put a hand on her shoulder to let her know she was there. Then after a while she went to get the cakes out of the oven. A delicious smell spread through the kitchen. The sudden normalcy calmed Erin down. She sat up and took a couple of deep breaths. She felt better now that she had let it all out. April smiled at her. "You can help me choose what to put on top. Peaches or pears."

"Peaches."

They decorated the cakes together and then April took Erin to her room to pick out some clothes for her. Erin freshened herself up in the bathroom and took off the wedding dress. As it lay on the floor, it felt like a second skin she had shed, a cocoon she'd crawled out of. She was a different creature now. No longer a woman who needed a man, who longed for love or a home. No. She was an independent woman who could make it on her own. Who had to take charge of her own life and fulfill her own dreams.

She put the dress away in a plastic bag beside the bed she was going to sleep in for the next few days. For her stay here. It was good to stay with someone she knew even just a little. To have something to talk about. Something other than her broken hopes and dreams.

As she came into the kitchen, April was just putting down her phone. "I texted my sister that I would be a little later. I promised to drop by to see the kids and have cake together. You can come along, if you want to?"

Erin hesitated. April said, "We need not tell her why you are here exactly. Just that we know each other from cruising and you are here for a short stay. Okay?"

Erin nodded. If she stayed here, holed up in her room, with that plastic bag holding her discarded wedding dress, she would sink back into sadness again. She needed some kind of diversion.

April said, "Good. You get the cakes and I will start the car."

After a short drive they arrived at the Williams Orchard Ranch. Erin remembered that April had once told her about the place where she had grown up but she had never imagined it would be so beautiful. So spacious and lush.

With the large ranch house and the cute little details like pots of flowers hanging from the porch. She could also hear animals in the barn and a border collie ran to meet them. She patted the dog with a smile. "That's Rosie, my brother Cade's dog," April explained. "She was bred by Wayne. He has the best cattle dogs in the district."

Erin brushed the dog's head. Those amber eyes looked like they understood a lot. It was as if Rosie sensed that Erin felt a little uncomfortable because she stayed by her side and guided her into the house.

April greeted a middle-aged woman with a hug and kisses. "Mom! This is Erin, a friend from my cruising days. She dropped by for a stay. I asked her to come along and see the place where I grew up. She heard so much about it from me."

Mrs. Williams shook Erin's hand. "Welcome to the ranch. You must have a look around later. See the orchards and the animals we keep. But first we will try the cakes."

"Is Gina not here?" April asked.

"She will be in a moment. She is getting the girls changed out of their dirty overalls. And little Barry is in his playpen."

April walked over to the playpen in a corner

of the kitchen and lifted out a cute little boy. "Hello there. You always keep so quiet. I can never tell whether you are there or not. Hello, little guy."

Erin's throat clogged up. She had wanted to get married and raise a family. She had imagined herself having kids with Hutch. A boy who looked just like him and would play football with Daddy. A little girl to dress up in cute white lace dresses and buy a dollhouse for. She had seen it all clearly in her wishful mind. Now the dream of having a little family was snatched away.

Mrs. Williams was cutting the cakes at the sink. April gestured for Erin to take a seat at the long table. Here was a home for family life. Sitting together, eating and talking, sharing, feeling a part of something bigger than yourself. But Erin had decided that wasn't to be for her. She'd stay on her own from now on, avoiding attachments. It was just too painful to be betrayed, made fun of as if you were a little child who didn't catch on. And perhaps she had been naive. Full of romantic nonsense that didn't hold up in real life. She had to shape up and focus on something new.

But what? She had quit cruising, the job

Hutch had gotten her at the flower shop was gone with him. What could she do?

Go back home, a voice whispered. *Make your parents happy. They always wanted you to be in the business with them. Now you can do that. Then at least you will be a good daughter. A good sister.*

April passed around plates and coffee mugs. A little girl's voice rang out and then two girls ran into the kitchen, wearing matching dresses. "These two are Stacey and Ann," April said, catching them in a big hug. "They are the cutest girls in the world. Go say hi to Erin. She is a friend of mine."

One girl stayed close to April looking at Erin with a shy smile but the other ran up to her, stood with feet planted apart and said, "Hi, I'm Stacey. Do you work on a big ship like April did? I want to go on one some day, see the world. Alaska and Japan. Faraway places."

"Stacey can't get far away enough, right?" April teased.

Erin smiled at the little girl. "I have been to both those places. I can tell you about them."

"Great."

Two women walked in and April introduced them as her sister Gina and sister-in-law Lily. Erin tried to keep straight who was who in the family. Lily sat down and got a mug of tea while all the others drank coffee. "That is for the baby," Stacey explained. "The baby doesn't like coffee."

They all laughed.

"Isn't Cade in?" April asked, pointing at her cakes. "I thought he would love this."

"He's in the orchard," Lily said, "should be back any minute now."

As she said it, male voices resounded outside. A tall dark man walked in, immediately looking at Lily and smiling widely. She waved at him and then at the cakes. "Your favorite."

But Erin didn't watch the cute gestures. Her gaze stayed firmly on the second man. Wayne. She had expected to meet him again during her stay here as this was obviously a small community, but so soon?

He met her eye with reluctance as if he also realized this was awkward. Cade was at the tap washing his hands. He urged his buddy to do the same so they could get started on the sweet treats.

As they sat down, Wayne opposite Erin, she glanced around the table and realized that this was how happy families looked. Three generations gathered, adults and children, those who had built this place and those who were stepping up to continue the legacy. She shouldn't be here. She should be with her parents and Livia, doing her part for the family business. Her own choices to go cruising, to fall in love, had led her astray and only caused heartbreak. Following their lead was better, safer. Was what she should have done all along.

She drank her coffee without tasting it, tried the cake and said it was delicious without really caring. All she could think of was that her decisions had been terrible and she should have known better. That her parents had to be so disappointed and she would have to work hard to restore their faith in her. But she was willing. She had to do something to make it all better.

"So because of the baby and all, I'm doing a little less committee work," Cade was explaining to her. "And Wayne took over a lot from me."

"Nothing special," Wayne said with a dismissive gesture.

"Well, it is a lot of work with the anniversary celebrations all through July," Cade frowned. "We also have the Apple Fest in August. You will be sending so many emails, taking late-night calls and doing early-morning visits to participants that you will wish you had never offered your help."

"I know what I am doing," Wayne assured him. He focused on Erin and smiled at her. She did still see a little concern in his eyes as if he was figuring out how she was feeling. To be honest, this whole cozy gathering didn't make her feel any better. It was too much of a confrontation with what she had lost. With her own mistakes that had cost her so much. She lowered her head and stared into her coffee mug.

"You know what," April said, "Erin knows all about flowers. She could help out, Wayne, decorating the community building for the anniversary events and helping with the grand parade."

Wayne looked at April. "Your friend is here to relax and unwind, not to get involved in a lot of hassle."

April seemed to want to kick him under the table. "Erin doesn't want to go sightseeing all of the time. She likes to be busy, right, Erin?"

Erin nodded vaguely. "I could have a look sometime and offer my advice." She hoped Wayne would forget all about it later and not really expect her to help. How could she focus on flowers with her life in shambles?

"That's decided then," April said. "It will be fun. There will still be enough time to go horse riding and all."

"Oh you didn't mention to me you ride," Wayne said to Erin.

"It's been ages. As a girl I did ride a pony but since then..."

"Don't worry, you remember how it's done."

"And we can always go riding together," April said. "It will be fun."

Erin assumed she meant well and wanted to cheer her up but the last thing she wanted was to be dragged into a thousand activities just so she didn't have to think of Hutch and how their relationship had imploded.

"You will like it here," Cade said. "The Rocky Mountains are nearby. They are really beautiful, lots of wildlife to see. You must take a day trip."

April cast him a look as if she wanted to make him shut up, but Cade continued, unsuspecting, "There is a really nice visitor center with lots of information and hiking paths. Gina works there, she can show you around sometime, can't you, Gina?"

"Of course," Gina said at once. "The girls will also like to show you around the center's garden."

"Yes, there is braille on the signs there," Stacey said, "and you have to figure out which animals passed from tracks in the sand. It's really exciting."

"You can also look inside the gift shop," Ann added. "They have stuffed animals."

Erin smiled but her heart beat fast at the idea of ever having to go back to those mountains. She wanted to stay far away from them.

Cade finished his coffee and pushed away his plate. "That was delicious, April, but Wayne and I must really get on with the chores."

"He means," Wayne said, with a grimace, "that while I supposedly help him with chores, he can lecture me about everything I have to do when he's not around. Like I can't figure it out for myself."

His tone was teasing, but Erin noticed the rigidness in his shoulders. It wasn't nice when someone had little confidence in you and thought they could actually do a better job. She gave Wayne an encouraging smile. He stared at her a moment as if it had caught him by surprise, then he smiled as well and winked at her. She felt a little lighter. They had to support each other. It was a really odd situation but she had been taken in by some very nice people who were intent on making her feel better. She would of course have to get in touch with Mom and Dad soon and try to make up for all the mistakes she had made. But first she needed a little time to steel herself against all of these emotions. She didn't want to go to them like a blubbering mess, but like an adult who could make better choices than in the past. She needed some downtime to regroup. And these people were kind enough to take her in and help her out. To protect her from Hutch and his family. By now they should have realized she was really not coming back. She could just see the disgruntled faces and hear the snide comments about her. Everybody would have to fly back home without having had the party they'd come for. But that was the way it was. Hutch was to blame, not her. She had to keep her back straight and live through this painful day. Tomorrow it would be a little easier.

She hoped.

CHAPTER FOUR

WHEN THEY HAD finished their coffee and cakes, April offered to show Erin around the ranch. "You have to see our flower fields," she said. "You will love them."

Erin smiled at her. "I already saw a little when we drove up to the house. Dahlias, right? They are gorgeous, easy to work with too. I love to put them in bouquets. Whether you use a whole bunch or single flowers in separate vases, they always look good on tables and reception desks."

"Cade grows many varieties," April said. "Let's walk out there to see them."

Mrs. Williams was gathering the dirty mugs and plates. Gina offered to help her wash them. The girls asked whether they could come to see the flowers too. April nodded and waved them along out the back door. Erin said, "You have a lovely family. Really warm and welcoming."

April glanced at her. She didn't know much

about Erin's family. In fact, she didn't know anything beyond the fact that they did something in real estate. She asked carefully, "Do you have any siblings?"

Erin nodded. "A big sister. Livia. She helps Mom and Dad in our family real estate firm. But she also does party planning. She likes to be busy and she is really good at what she does."

April looked at the girls, who ran ahead of them waving their arms. "I grew up with both a big brother and a big sister. Being youngest was fun in ways because everybody cared for me and looked after me and spoiled me. But it was also…complicated sometimes. I was always little April, the Williams girl. The one with the ponytails and the overalls. I never truly grew up."

"I know what you mean." Erin grimaced. "Livia can be a bit overbearing. She always thinks she knows what is best. She is good at what she does, like I just said, so I guess she has a lot of reasons to be proud and think she is doing everything right but… As girls we used to be pretty close, always playing together and thinking up fun games. But later we grew more distant. These days…" She sighed heavily. "Livia wasn't happy when I decided on a career in cruising. She had always thought I would help with the family business. Like she does."

"We can't all do the same thing. I grew up on the ranch here and I love outdoor living, but when my father died, I felt sort of…detached. Cade took over from him taking care of the ranch alongside Mom and… I went into cruising. I did it to get away from here, from the grief I felt, but soon it developed into the kind of career I really wanted."

"Still, you gave it all up to marry." Erin said it softly, with a sad expression.

April was sorry that her attempt at conversation had led right back to the unwanted topic. To the shame and embarrassment Erin had to be feeling over her failed wedding. "It was hard. I was newly promoted to officer. I wasn't ready to just throw it all away. But sometimes feelings are bigger than…"

"Common sense?" Erin supplied. "Livia told me many times how I was letting my feelings rule my life. That I was making the biggest mistake ever by falling for Hutch. The more she said it, the less I listened. I wanted to push on to show her it could work."

"And because you loved him, right?" April asked gently. "You didn't decide to marry him to spite your sister. You cared for him. Which is nothing to feel bad about. That he wasn't worth it is his fault, not yours."

Erin sighed as she swung her hands by her side. "You know, looking back now I am just not sure how much of my determination to push on with this was love for Hutch and how much was a need to show my family I could make my own decisions. Right decisions. They always treat me like…that little kid who can't walk on her own without falling over. I needed to show them that… I have my life under control. Well…" She pulled a face. "They will certainly believe that after today. I mean, they don't know yet, but they will."

"They don't know yet that you aren't married? So they weren't there?" April queried. She sensed that Erin wanted to talk about this, had to talk about it, get it off her chest.

Erin shook her head. "I didn't invite them. It seemed better to avoid conflict. They never liked Hutch and…it all seemed like a good idea. To keep them out of it and just make my own decisions. For my future. But apparently I can't make the right ones. I was so wrong about Hutch. Or maybe the sad conclusion has to be that I knew deep down inside that he wasn't honest or reliable and still I pushed on. Even this morning when I stood in front of the mirror looking at my dress, I knew it wasn't what I had wanted and still I didn't see a way out."

April didn't know quite what to say. She had at first assumed Erin was heartbroken because of the betrayal, of losing the man she had loved without question. But it now seemed to be more complicated. Erin had felt doubts but not allowed herself to act on them. She had become the victim because she had waited too long to do anything. That probably made the situation even worse for her. To realize that she herself had played a part in the unhappy ending to the big day.

April touched her arm. "You shouldn't blame yourself. I mean, things are sometimes not that clear. You need time to figure out how you feel and what you want. It can be easy to be swept away and… I had the same thing when I came back here and stayed with Matt. I was on leave and I had come home to see Gina's baby. Barry was three months old, an adorable little kid. I was all squishy because he was so sweet and he reminded me of my own dreams of marriage and family. So when I started to have feelings for Matt, I questioned myself whether it was just a phase I was going through, fake feelings or the real thing. It was hard because…he was sort of my teenage crush. It was like I was going back to being that blushing girl and he didn't have a clue. I dealt with a lot of conflicting emotions that didn't have to do with Matt per se but with me. What I wanted. Who I was. How people saw me and what I wanted them to see. Maybe you also need a little distance to check in with yourself and ask what you want to do next. Go back to cruising or start a career in flowers." She gestured ahead to the colorful dahlia fields. "Those have your heart."

Erin smiled. "They sure do. Whenever I see flowers, I forget everything around me and I just want to dive in and make gorgeous creations. They make me happy in ways I can't explain. They mean so much to me that… I even gave up my place in the family business for them." Her smile faded. "My parents were upset about that. Disappointed in me. Maybe it's time to make amends. To go back to them and do what they always wanted me to. I mean, I had my time to run free. See the world, go explore exciting cities, meet new people. It was nice but…life isn't all about doing nice things. It is also about obligation. Duty. Responsibility."

April was surprised by Erin's sudden revelation about her possible return to the family business. But she suspected there was more behind this than just the shock of having discovered Hutch's infidelity. Maybe Erin had always struggled with her sense of guilt, of having let down her parents who had expected so much of her. "You don't have to decide overnight. Take a little time to refocus. I mean, for the first few days you shouldn't think about the past or the future at all. Just live in the present. Give yourself a chance to heal a little. You won't just forget what happened but you can put it in perspective. If you already had doubts about Hutch..."

"I had heard the rumors about why he was fired but just didn't want to believe them. He always reassured me that everything was fine. That the accusations were false because people misinterpreted his easygoing ways. Or because the captain was shielding someone else. He made it all sound so plausible. Everything always turned out the way he wanted it to. He found a buddy to start a business with once he left the ship. Rented an apartment for us in a desirable location with few vacancies. Life was always kind to him. Favored him. He was sort of a golden boy and everyone wanted to be near him."

Erin smiled sadly. "I am talking about him

in the past tense as if he is no longer there. But he is. He is continuing his life, without me." She swallowed a moment. "It won't be with the woman he betrayed me with, I suspect. Maybe for a while but not for long. I see now that to him it's only interesting while there is still something left to gain. To go after. To hunt for. Then once he has it all, I assume the thrill is over and he has to go after something new."

"I am sorry that you fell in love with someone who doesn't deserve you," April said. "I want something much better for you. When we worked together on the ship, I saw how kind you were to others. You filled in for them or helped them out. You were always giving people the best of you. Now it's time you are on the receiving end of some kindness."

Erin seemed to find these compliments almost painful and made a dismissive gesture with her hand. But April pushed on and said, "It's true. You have a good heart and you should never settle for anything less than someone who totally loves you for you. Who would do anything to be with you. For whom you would do the same."

Erin laughed bitterly. "I was so in love with Hutch I even risked my relationship with my family for him. I agreed to marry him without them present. I betrayed them. Once they find out, they will be so hurt and angry. I lost my dream of love but I also lost them too."

"No, you mustn't see it that way." April touched her arm again. "They'll understand. They'll be glad the wedding didn't go through and they will support you."

"I'm not so sure."

"Look!" Stacey had run into the field of flowers and was standing beside a large white dahlia. "It is as tall as I am."

"Careful, girls," April warned, "those flowers have to be sold. You can walk among them but don't touch them and don't be wild."

Erin gingerly stepped over to a multicolored flower and smiled up at it. "It's beautiful. You have so many varieties here. Colors, shapes. They're like a garden to me where I want to walk around and freely pick whatever I like."

"You can't pick them." Stacey wagged a finger at her. "They're Uncle Cade's flowers. He has to sell them."

Her serious expression made them all laugh. Stacey looked hurt. "It is true," she insisted.

"Yes, it is, munchkin," April said brushing the little girl's hair away from her forehead. "Erin won't pick any. Not yet anyway." She looked around her with a sudden idea. "But she might be doing so soon."

ERIN BLINKED AT APRIL. "Sorry?" Her head was so full of conflicting emotions it almost banged. On the one hand she was visiting this gorgeous ranch where they grew flowers and it was like a favorite outing on a summer's day. On the other hand, she had lost the entire future she had planned and despite the bright sunshine she felt like she stood here in the pouring rain.

April said, "We just talked about the town anniversary celebrations. Wayne has so much to organize for them but we could take a little load off his shoulders. You can decorate the community center with flowers. These flowers. You make the most amazing creations. It will be wonderful." She leaned over and added, "And distracting. You don't want to sit around and feel glum all day long."

Erin had to agree it would be good to do something. Anything. And if it involved flowers, it was all the better. Also, it would be like a return favor to Wayne who had been so kind to her when she had needed to flee the resort. Working with flowers soothed her mind. It would calm her tangled emotions and prepare her for thinking up a way to make up with her parents and Livia. Flowers had always been her joy, a healing balm when life was rough.

She took a deep breath. The girls were running among the flowers, their high-pitched voices drifting toward April and her. The sun shone down and cast every single flower in bright light. Made the colors seem more vivid and the shapes more pronounced. She stood in a place of such natural beauty it took her breath away. And she could actually stay here for a while and work with these flowers. What was not to like?

She turned to April and said, “Why are you being so nice to me when I have just landed on your doorstep in my wedding dress? It feels like… I don’t know. I should be crying because the worst happened and still when I am standing in this field, I feel almost…blessed that I ended up here. With these beauties and with you all. You are so friendly and…”

She had really needed a bit of kindness. She sensed that sharply now. There had been a lot happening at the resort with Hutch’s extended family and friends. Lots of emotions in evidence, but kindness and love weren’t among them. The guests had all been busy with their clothes and rooms and with drinking and telling big tales of where they had vacationed. They had been full of themselves, but none of them had been truly interested in her. They had all treated her like she was…not that important. While she was the bride. A key player.

April said softly, "You don't need to thank any of us for just being kind to you, Erin. You deserve that." Her eyes were worried as she studied her. "Have you felt that alone? That is not right. Who were these people who said they were your friends?"

Erin shrugged. Tears burned in her eyes anew. "I don't know," she said, a feeling of helplessness washing over her. "I don't know."

"Come here." April reached out and wrapped her arms around her. "You are safe now. We will look after you."

Erin rested her head on April's shoulder and cried.

WAYNE STEERED HIS TRUCK down the road to go and get the lumber Cade needed for a small repair to his barn. They would finish the job together and then they could barbeque, Cade had said. Wayne was always interested in a nice burger, especially if he didn't have to cook it himself. And maybe he'd see a little more of Erin too. He imagined April would also want to stay for the barbeque. Or would she be going back to the hotel? In that case, Erin could stay on the ranch and Wayne would drive her back later. That would really be no trouble.

He passed the flower fields and looked with a smile as Stacey and Ann played among the flowers. Then he saw something else, something that made his heart stop a moment and then pound heavily. Two women hugged each other tightly. April and Erin. Judging by her shaking shoulders, Erin was sobbing her heart out. She had to have really loved that guy. Thought they would be together for the rest of their lives. She had wanted to make a commitment, say I do. But her fiance had betrayed her, left her out in the cold. Her heart was broken. Nothing they could do about that.

April had to feel so helpless, at a loss what to say or do.

Wayne drove on quickly, glad they hadn't seen him. He was useless when it came to dealing with emotions. Like his father and his brother Alex had been. They had all been devastated when his mother had died. Left in a house from which the heart had disappeared. But they hadn't said it. Neither of them. His dad had probably felt the need to look strong for his sons. Alex had always gone to friends after school and stayed there for dinner, as if to avoid the emptiness at home. And when Wayne then ate with his dad, in a suffocating silence, he had felt like he shouldn't make it harder on Dad by crying or asking questions about where Mom was now and if she was happy. They all had to try their best to carry on.

The elderly neighbor had said so. A little old lady who had taken him aside and told him to be brave now that his mother had passed away, to make it easy on his father. *Be a good boy and don't cry or create mischief.*

Oh, he had listened alright. He had tried his very best to be the son his father wanted. But somehow it hadn't worked out.

Wayne clenched the wheel. It didn't matter anymore. Dad at least had one son he could be proud of. A successful lawyer in NYC. Dad had even moved away from Heartmont to be closer to Alex and his family. Alex had it all: the college degree, the high-flying job, the beautiful wife and the cute little kids. He had become what Dad wanted. What Mom had wanted too, probably. Who cared for a bachelor with a patch of land, a farmhouse where things broke down regularly, a few cows, a few puppies? No wife, no children. At his age you had to have something to show off, to prove you had worked hard to make a success of your life.

He guessed he had failed the elderly neighbor after all. He had not been the good boy he was supposed to have been. It wasn't like it bothered him day and night. Nope. He liked his life and he didn't care what other people thought of it. He had learned, the hard way, not to feel too much. Or maybe not to feel anything. It was better that way. Just think of poor Erin crying her heart out. All because she had allowed herself to love someone who wasn't worth it.

He was mad at that guy. Mad enough to drive to that mountain resort and tell him the truth. That he was a lousy loser who should be ashamed of himself.

But guys like that never learnt a lesson. They went on to hurt new people. At least it wouldn't be Erin anymore.

She was safe now with them. They would keep her here for a while and help her feel better. Recuperate. April had suggested something about her helping him with the anniversary celebrations. A nice distraction. And horse riding maybe. He could of course also invite her to his house to see the puppies. Little dogs always made people smile. And his were the cutest in the county.

It made him feel better to make a plan to help her. He lived for to-do lists and activities. That was why having a ranch was great. There was so much to do. From dawn to dusk he was busy taking care of his animals and his land, then helping neighbors and driving into town for supplies or the next meeting about the town anniversary celebrations. He could run around all day long and never have a dull moment. Never sit down to stare across his land and wonder how it all would have turned out if he had followed his father's advice. If he had also gone to college and become a lawyer, would he have a wife now and kids?

You didn't need to be a city slicker with an office job to find a wife. But then he had to draw another conclusion. It wasn't his profession or living in a small town where you just didn't meet too many new people. No. It was him.

Even Cade had found love. His best buddy, the confirmed bachelor who lived for his orchards and agility training with Rosie the border collie. Cade had fallen in love and now he was becoming a father.

It made Wayne a little nostalgic. Soon he

would be the only bachelor left among his friends. The last man standing. He tried to laugh but his expression stayed serious. People thought he liked to be alone. He had even told himself that lie. But he wasn't alone by choice. He was alone because he wasn't cut out for companionship. Because the past had changed him, his childhood had shaped him, and it didn't seem like any amount of adult intervention could turn that around. It was easy for him to flirt with women in a casual way, give them a wink or a compliment, dance with them at a barn party, even have a dinner at the steakhouse. But he never could quite see how to move on from there. You needed to open up and share things and… It was just not his way.

Why was he even thinking about all of this? Another person's failed wedding, making him all sentimental? It was not like he had been stood up at the altar. No. He would never make it to the altar. No one would ever want to take a chance on him. He wouldn't ask it either. It just wouldn't be fair. Women needed a different type of man. Kind and caring and…talkative. He knew he would just not fit the bill. So it had to be him and his dog and his cows. For the rest of his life.

Was that sad? Or was it rather reassuring?

The animals didn't expect anything of him beyond care. He fed them and petted them and cared for their injuries and their ailments. He knew them inside out and they rewarded him with their trust. They never asked hard questions and they were never disappointed. It was ideal.

Still, as he drove away from that flower field where the women hugged each other tightly, putting more and more distance between himself and that uncomfortable little scene, he felt like the reality was somehow different than he had always led himself to believe. That human relationships were maybe a bigger part of life than he had wanted to acknowledge so far. And that meant nothing but trouble.

CHAPTER FIVE

WHEN ERIN AND April came back from looking at the flower fields, Erin immediately spotted the big barbeque in the yard. Cade was standing by it, putting coals under the grate. Lily walked out of the house with a tray full of plates and he went over to take it from her and place it on a table. She shook her head but there was a tenderness in her eyes. This was what love looked like. Seeing another's need and stepping up to meet it. Doing it without even thinking about it. Because you cared.

Erin swallowed hard. She had never had that with Hutch. Hutch had taken her out to dinner and given her presents, yes, he had looked like he cared in that respect. But all of that had been to impress her, and more often others. He wanted them to think he had money and could treat his girlfriend to the best things in life. It was all a show.

A show she no longer wanted or needed to

be a part of. It was sad that their relationship had ended the way it had, but it was also a relief. Because she had not been able to be herself with him. When they had first met, she had figured he was this charming man who was too good for her. And it was actually a big surprise he had liked her at all. She had believed she should be grateful because he had chosen her even though she didn't deserve it.

That was so wrong. It formed the base for a toxic relationship in which one party was always catering to the other to earn affection. She had known that to be true, but she had not recognized it when it had happened to her. She had idealized their meeting, had found the whole *I chose you* thing romantic. Now she saw sharply what it had really been like. How being with Hutch had constantly undermined her self-confidence. How he had not lifted her up but put her down, keeping the doubts alive about whether she was good enough for him. She wished with all of her heart that she had met someone like Cade who was kind and good to everyone around him. Who had a giving nature instead of a taking one.

But that was all over now. She had been hurt by Hutch and she had not even seen the risk. She had been misled by her feelings, her hopes and dreams. She would not be so careless again. She would now carefully guard her heart. And make something of her life on her own.

Cade saw April and her coming with the children. He waved. "We're putting together an impromptu barbeque. Just for fun. There was lots in the fridge we could use. And we hope you will stay to join in."

"I don't want you to go to any trouble for me," Erin said.

April squeezed her arm. "It's no trouble. Cade likes any excuse to grill meat. He and Wayne have been working hard today so it will be a nice way to unwind."

Wayne!

Erin had almost forgotten about him. She had figured he would be long gone by now. But there he was coming from the kitchen, rubbing his hands as if he had just washed and dried them. He looked at her and there was this odd feeling in the pit of her stomach. He had seen her when she had been so undone. At her lowest, ready to run away from what was supposed to have been the happiest day of her life. Even now that she no longer wore the hated dress and had become part of this group of friendly people, she felt exposed. He had overheard the phone call, he had seen her cry. It was all so odd. Normally when you met new people, they saw you as able and capable of handling your life.

Wayne came over with long strides and smiled at her. "How did you like the flowers? Cade has lots of them. I don't know what all of them are called but people love them. We can use them for decorations for the anniversary celebrations. I have no idea how to work with flowers so it would be great if you could give me some pointers like April suggested earlier. You know, expert advice?"

She hardly felt like an expert now. In the flower fields she had felt a spark of hope she could work through her emotions by distraction, but as she pictured herself giving advice while she felt like the least capable person in the district, her heart sank. She looked down and shuffled her feet.

He said, "I understand if you would rather have time to yourself. But the celebrations are taking up a lot of my work time and every helping hand is more than welcome. If you could just look at the venue, and give some tips… Tomorrow maybe?"

She took a deep breath and came to a decision. He had been very helpful when she needed it and she also wanted to repay April and her family for their hospitality. "Okay. Just let me know when you will come to pick me up." She scribbled down her phone number on a napkin and gave it to him. It reminded her that she would have to turn her phone back on, but not right now. Later tonight or tomorrow morning when she woke up. She supposed that there would be people who wanted to talk to her. The manager at the wedding venue for instance, about the expenses for the party that had not taken place. Everything had been ready and waiting. She would still have to pay a steep cancellation fee. How sour was that, how unfair also. But for now she wanted to ignore her troubles.

"Perfect, thanks," he said as he tucked the napkin with the phone number in his pocket. "Is there something you'd like to eat? A little salad to start with? Lettuce, tomatoes, olives, there is lots."

"I'll go and have a look." She hadn't eaten much today and her stomach was growling. She walked with him to the long table where food was ready. He handed her a plate and she selected something out of every bowl. It all looked so delicious. And the atmosphere was so relaxed. If she had still been at the resort, if she had married and had been Mrs. Michaels now, there would be a big fancy dinner with dancing afterward. All in grand style. It seemed now like it would have been stressful rather than pleasant. Those fancy affairs had been a regular part of her life when she still worked in her parents' company. They had thrown parties for their business relations and attended parties in return. Occasions where she had to dress up and look her finest, make charming conversation, be bright and funny. She had been used to it, hadn't regarded it as a chore. She was probably just tired now and therefore feeling like socializing was always a little like performing and having to be perfect.

"Can you get me some tomatoes with feta?" Stacey asked. She looked up at Erin with a wide grin. "You are much taller than me. I like your dress."

Erin was painfully conscious it was April's dress, but she didn't say so. "Thanks for the compliment."

"I heard Mom say you work with flowers," Stacey continued. "What do you do with them?"

"I make bouquets and floral displays. Like when people are celebrating a birthday or anniversary, then I decorate the room. Maybe I'll twine roses into chairs or make bouquets to go on the table. It is a lot of fun and always very rewarding. People like what I make."

"That must be nice. Can you teach me how to do it? I would like to be able to do something fun. Ann is always crafting with cork and paperboard. But I don't like that. It's too fiddly."

"I could show you a few things. But flowers are very delicate so you will have to be gentle."

"I will be. I can be when I want to." Stacey accepted the plate she had filled with tomatoes and feta. "Thanks." The little girl turned away and then turned back to her. "Have you seen our donkeys? They are very sweet. I can show you..."

"First we are all going to eat something," Gina said. She had approached them without Erin noticing. "You can show Erin later. She will be staying for some time so there is no rush."

Stacey nodded and darted off to meet Ann who had seated herself on the swinging bench on the porch. Gina said to Erin, "My daughters can be quite a handful when they are demanding attention. It's perfectly okay to tell them no if you don't feel up to doing what they want." Her eyes searched Erin's expression as if she wanted to see how she really felt right now.

Erin forced a smile. “It’s fine. A nice diversion. You have a beautiful place here. You must have loved it growing up.”

Gina nodded. “We always had animals to play with. And we did hide-and-seek in the orchards. Being outdoors most of the time was a nice way to grow up.”

Erin tasted her salad. She had never been outdoors much as a child. Her parents had been fully immersed in city life. They had taken them to restaurants and parties and on holiday they had visited museums rather than gone hiking. It had fed her interest in history and later during cruises she had taken every opportunity to see more of other cultures and their traditions. Traveling was so rewarding. To think she had almost given up on that for Hutch… Now that she had broken up with him, she had to make sure travel stayed a big part of her life. Seeing exciting places and diving into another lifestyle. Even as a little girl she had tasted oysters and other seafood, special ingredients like truffles and saffron, at the restaurants where Mom and Dad took her and Livia. They had been expected to try new foods and acquire a taste for the finest. Expensive, exclusive. Those were the words her parents also used for the properties they sold. Their entire lives were based on going after the extraordinary. Something like this outdoor BBQ would be much too simple for them.

"The first burgers are ready," Cade called and she walked over to get one. He was wearing a leather apron and worked the spatula with skill. He was right at home here. Of course this was his home but she felt he fitted perfectly in these surroundings. He was in place here.

Had she ever felt that way? Or had she always been looking for a way to belong? In her parents' high-class world, status and money were everything, being able to show off what you had. On the cruise ship she had had to learn a lot in a short span of time and it had kept her on her toes, always afraid to fall short.

Yes, that was it. Despite all the opportunities given to her, first by her parents, then cruise ship life, she had often felt she always had to deliver what others wanted, be who they wanted her to be. But who was she really and what would she be doing if the choice were totally up to her and her alone?

"Are you okay?" Wayne asked. He stood beside her, eyeing her with worry in his eyes. "You have had a hard day."

"It's okay," she rushed to say. Her mind was spinning with the realization she was free now to make her own choices. It was a daunting idea. Could she even make the right choices? Or would she always doubt herself? The disaster with Hutch proved she was easily deceived by her feelings. "I am just tired. I need to sit down and eat."

He nodded and led her to a table with a bench beside it, a little away from the others who were around the barbeque watching Cade flip the burgers. Wayne gestured for her to sit. "Can I get you a drink? Lemonade? Homemade, really nice."

"Sure."

She watched him as he walked away, at ease here. This place had to be like a second home to him, because he had called Cade his best buddy. They had probably been close since school. It seemed things were a given here, no questions asked.

This was a community where people were tight, supportive and relaxed. It was a nice environment, and somewhere where nothing was expected of her. In fact, it seemed like everyone was just totally okay with the fact she had dropped in. Her parents would be upset if someone showed up unexpected. They would of course get a room ready, they had a housekeeper to do that, and they would order the best food and exclusive wines to treat their guest but…they would still be uncomfortable with the intrusion. Here it seemed that anyone driving into the yard could join in. Grab a plate and have a burger. There was more than enough.

"There you go." Wayne put the glass of lemonade beside her plate. He hovered over her like a protective force. "Anything else?"

"Not right now. Why don't you sit with me? Have you got any food yet?"

"Let me get some…" Wayne walked off again, joining the group and making a joke here and there. He quickly returned with a plate with three burgers on it and a little salad.

"You must be hungry," she observed.

He shrugged. "I have been doing manual labor all day long. That works up an appetite. Cade had me drive into town to get lumber. His barn needed a few repairs."

"It must be a real plus to be good with your hands. I can't repair anything around my home. I mean, my previous apartment had someone to do chores but…" She had only been at the apartment when she was on leave from cruising. It hadn't felt like a true home. She hadn't been sorry to pack up her things and put them in storage until the apartment was ready where she was going to live with Hutch, after their wedding and honeymoon.

She actually didn't have a home right now. No street address. She was suspended between her old life and something new she'd have to devise, and fast. The idea took her breath away and not in a good way. She gripped her plate, focusing on the topic of conversation to divert herself from the rising panic inside. "…it seems like it would be convenient to be able to do something myself. You know. Not have to hire someone all of the time." It would be nice to feel competent, good at something.

"Oh, I could teach you a few things." Wayne took a bite and chewed. Having swallowed, he continued, "How to repair a leaky faucet or an unhinged door… It's not that hard once you know how to do it."

Erin sighed. "That's like life, huh? It is not too hard once you know how to do it. Only thing is, do you ever know how to do it?" She moved her olives around on her plate. She just couldn't stop thinking about how naive she had been to pack up her entire life for Hutch. Quit her job, the apartment. She had nothing left to go back to.

Wayne ate in silence for a few moments. She thought he had barely heard her observation.

Which was kind of weird and pointless anyway. Why had she even said it? This was a night for chitchat, small talk, not for deep conversations about life.

Then he said, "I don't think I ever figured it out. Or ever will for that matter. It's like every time things have sort of settled down, there comes another curveball your way. But you can't get away from it. It is your life. Always will be. Can't ask someone else to live it for you."

She eyed him with curiosity. On the outside it seemed he was someone who took life easy. Who would never ask too many hard questions. Why would he anyway, when he had it all worked out, running his ranch and having a good time with his friends when work was done. His unexpected honesty warmed her deep inside. Others faced the same dilemmas and weren't afraid to admit it.

Wayne shrugged. "Maybe you think it's kind of odd to even think about doing something like that. To take a break from your life. Just go away and let someone else deal with the mess for a while."

That sounded pretty amazing. A solution she'd take in a heartbeat.

"You just go on a holiday," he said, "and

come back when everything's all in order. Bright and shiny. Perfect."

"You need a perfect life?" she inquired gently.

He grimaced. "Not for me. Family expectations."

"Oh." She could relate to that. "But uh…this is a ranching community, right? What expectations are there?"

He winced. "You think just like my father. Ranchers have no real work, no job worth speaking of."

"I never said that."

She cringed under the judgment implied, but Wayne continued, "My father thinks that nobody wants to be a rancher if he has half a choice. People here have to take over family ranches. That's usually why they do it. But if they had a little bit of ambition, they'd move away and do something else. You know. That's his way of looking at it and he can't be persuaded to see it any differently."

"I see." She tried to figure out why his father would feel that way. "Did he himself not have a choice to become something other than a rancher?"

"My dad was no rancher. We did live here, in town, but he ran the local bookshop. He was also on the city council. He always wanted to move up in life." Wayne chewed in silence for a few moments before adding, "He wanted a good life for his boys. Alex and me. He did everything to make that possible for us. Invested in our education. But I was never a book person. Didn't like reading. Or school. During lessons I stared out of the window wishing that bell rang and I could run outside to play ball or go horse riding. My grades were always just good enough to get by, but… He was often angry, telling me that I didn't try hard enough. That I could do better if I only wanted it. He tried all kinds of methods with me. Being nice and saying I was so smart and should just show it. Or telling me I was lazy and unambitious and would never amount to anything unless I tried harder. He hoped that some reverse psychology would do the trick. But I never changed. No matter what he tried." He shrugged. "My attitude as he called it was a big setback for him. It wasn't how he had wanted to raise me. When I decided not to go to college but to travel a bit, try ranching in other parts of the world, he was…really really mad at me."

"I see." She sensed that Wayne downplayed his father's reaction. She wanted to know more about how this anger had shown itself but as they barely knew each other, she couldn't really ask. "But you did come back here."

"Yes, I earned money abroad and then I came back and bought this patch of land nobody wanted and I worked hard to make something of it. Built my own house. Plank by plank. One barn, then another. Got a cow that was about to have a calf. The calf happened to be female, so that was two cows..." He laughed softly. "It was a long road. But I liked it. Maybe like you do with flowers. Create something of your own making."

Erin nodded although it seemed hardly the same. She did floral arrangements for others who paid her. She only had to invest her time, not risk her savings or anything. He had built a ranch with his own bare hands. He had taken the chance of it going wrong, of losing everything. He had to be very courageous. And strong-willed. To have gone against his father...

"Does he still have the bookshop in town? Your father?"

"No, he sold it a while back. He moved to NYC to be closer to my brother and his family. Dad wanted to see the grandkids grow up."

"I understand. My parents have been pressuring me and Livia, my sister, to get married and give them grandkids. Too bad for them that neither of us is in a rush. I mean, Livia is a real career woman and I…" Her voice trailed off.

Wayne said quickly, "I'm glad for Dad that he has family around, you know. He must have been lonely through the years."

"Your mother…" she asked carefully.

"Died when I was little. I never really knew her." It sounded detached. Maybe he had said those words so many times it had become as normal as mentioning his date of birth. Still… Growing up without one of his parents had to have had some impact on his life.

"I see. That must be hard."

"It's not hard when you don't know anything else than just being with your dad and brother." He spoke in a matter-of-fact way, then got up. "I'm going to get some more food. You?"

"I've only just started. Thanks." She tilted her head as she watched him walk away again. He was so different from any other man she had ever met. She didn't know anyone who had built their own house. Who worked with his hands all the time. Who had made radical decisions to do things differently than his family had. She had always felt like the outlier with her choices, but they were nothing compared to

Wayne's path in life. He didn't seem to care at all that his father hadn't been happy with him or that he had moved away to spend all of his time with Wayne's brother and his family. She bet she would feel left out if her parents were fully focused on Livia.

Would feel left out? Or was she already in that position? They loved Livia for being part of the company. She always did what they wanted. She was the good girl while Erin had become the prodigal daughter. The one who needed to come home.

And now her new life had fallen apart and she could indeed turn back. But would she? She didn't feel like returning with her tail between her legs. As if her choices had been all wrong.

They might seem to have been. Choosing Hutch anyway. But her other decisions? The cruising, the distance she'd needed to work out what she wanted, apart from them? Was that so wrong? Should she throw in the towel and go back, or try for something else? Knowing that she might fail again?

The mere idea made her stomach contract. She was so raw from today's shock. She could not face another disaster. Right now she was ready to pack everything in and hide for the rest of her life. But that wasn't realistic, of course.

She did need to think up a way to deal with her wedding fiasco. It was a good thing April had suggested to involve her in the anniversary celebrations here and Wayne had invited her to come and see the venue tomorrow. Now she had a reason, a valid business reason, to stay in Heartmont. If her parents contacted her for one of those casual "how are you?" phone calls, which they would hopefully not do, but if they did, she could claim to be here for work. That she had gotten an assignment via April whom she knew from cruising. Something plausible like that. They would appreciate that she was at least employed. Even if it was a temporary thing, and a world away from the life of status and wealth they had wanted for her.

It was hard to think of how much she had let them down. Part of her ached to make it up to them. Prove she could be everything they wanted her to be. To have their love and appreciation. Everybody needed that, right? It wasn't odd to want that. Even at her age.

But could she ever get it? She had let them down by her job choice, her relationship with Hutch. How could she ever convince them she knew what she was doing with her life if she couldn't even convince herself?

CHAPTER SIX

WAYNE WATCHED ERIN from beside the food buffet. He hadn't really wanted much more but he had needed a break from their sudden deep conversation. He couldn't remember when he had last talked to anyone about Dad. Or the time when his mother had died. Here she was, a perfect stranger who could just get him to open up to her. He hadn't felt offended by her questions. Maybe because she was so sad and lonely and he just wanted her to feel better?

Even as he stood watching her, it struck him how vulnerable she looked sitting there. She was here with a lot of people, but she had to feel like she was all alone in the world. Her fiancé had betrayed her, her wedding day had been brutally canceled, her plans for the future had been obliterated. Tomorrow morning she'd wake up and realize what had happened all over again. He could offer her work, a temporary diversion, but would it be enough? Would it do anything to cure the pain of her broken heart?

It made him angry to think of this guy who had wormed himself into her affections only to let her down. He had obviously never deserved her. But Erin probably didn't feel that way. She loved the guy. Had wanted to be with him for the rest of her life. Maybe inside she was crying for him. Even after people let you down and trampled your heart like his dad had, never accepting who he was, you could still think of them with that deep-seated wish that they had been there for you, despite it all. It was strange but true.

"Are you going to get something to eat or just stand there staring into space?" Cade's teasing voice tore him from his thoughts. Fortunately he said *staring into space*, not *staring at a beautiful woman.*

Cade probably hadn't noticed Erin was a beautiful woman. Cade only had eyes for Lily. From the day he had met her he had been in love with her, even if he had refused to admit it to himself. After they had gotten married, it had only become worse. Cade was busy all day long with what Lily wanted, how he could make the ranch more comfortable for her, from buying a calf she had seen and adored to thinking up some date they could go on. And now that Lily was pregnant, it was like there was nothing in the world for Cade but talking about how Lily needed rest, or what they could buy for a baby room or…

Yep, Wayne felt like he had sort of lost his buddy. Gone were the days where they went out for a beer and darts at the local grillroom. They didn't go hiking anymore. Let alone play music in their old high school band the Heartmont Heroes. He hadn't realized before but right now it was crystal clear to him that he missed that friendship. Times spent together to relax and unwind, to connect in a meaningful way. Cade getting married had made Wayne lonelier than ever.

"What is wrong with you?" Cade asked. "You look at me like you have never seen me before."

"I was just wondering: with the anniversary coming up, will the Heartmont Heroes play again?"

A tender look came into Cade's eyes. "Lily was fantastic right at our first renewed Apple Fest… That dress made her sparkle all over. And the look in her eyes… I guess I knew then that I wanted to marry her. Even if I didn't tell her yet."

Wayne resisted the urge to sigh. Every topic led back to Lily it seemed. "Look, I need to know if we will perform. You and me. For old times' sake." It would be the perfect excuse to get Cade to come over to his place for a few nights. They could chat, catch up. Wayne needed to feel they were still mates. Despite Cade's growing family responsibilities.

Cade shook his head. "I don't think so. Lily can't join in. I mean, I bet she would want to but I won't let her. She has to take it easy. And if we have to rehearse, I'd have to be away from home and… Just not a good idea. Maybe next year?"

Wayne nodded, deflated inside. Maybe next year… Yeah, sure. Cade would be busy with the baby and other stuff. There was always a reason. A reason why Wayne didn't fit into the equation anymore. Well, people did grow apart over time and maybe he just had to accept it. That they weren't the same men as they had been three years ago. Or ten.

Cade said, "Speaking of music, why don't you play a few tunes for us? I'll get my guitar for you." Without waiting for a reply he went inside.

Wayne wanted to say he didn't feel like it, had a headache or whatever, but he knew Cade would press him to do it anyway and it might help to shake his melancholy mood. He was just not himself tonight.

He went back to Erin. "Cade asked me to play a little music. He's getting his guitar. I'll be back with you later, okay? He really wants me to do this, so… I hope you like country music?"

Erin looked as if she was about to say she didn't really but felt it would be impolite. Cade had already come over to them with the guitar. Wayne accepted it and went to sit on a stool beside the buffet table. He strummed the guitar for a few moments to tune it and then looked around. Nobody was paying attention.

Yet.

With a smile he started to play.

ERIN HAD FELT kind of cornered by Wayne's question. She had never listened much to country music and associated it mainly with fiddles and hand clapping and line dancing. There was nothing wrong with that, but she had been raised by her parents to appreciate classical music, opera. Later they had taken Livia and her to Broadway to the big musicals. When she had been cruising, she had often taken the opportunity to attend classical concerts and operas abroad, often at special locations like a palace garden or in the courtyard of a medieval castle. Music was something grand and elevated to her, best enjoyed when you were all dressed up and with likeminded people. In a split second she had thought that what he was going to perform here might be a little too… ordinary for her taste?

She cringed again. First she had offended him when her question had led to him concluding she considered farming a lowly profession, like his father had. And now she was looking down on the music he played and probably enjoyed. Everything about these people was pure and authentic and still it felt like something she could never be a part of. As if she watched it all from behind a glass window she couldn't break through.

Wayne started his song softly, gently, his singing so subdued that she could see his lips move but not hear the words. She wanted to hear them but the others were talking and clanking their plates. However, Lily put her hand on Gina's arm and they fell silent and then Mrs. Williams noticed too, and even the kids stopped running around and looked at Wayne. He kept singing slowly and with emphasis about this lone cowboy who traveled the hills and looked to the west where the sun was setting. He asked himself the question of where he could lay his head down for the night. If there was a place where he would be safe and welcome. Or whether he would just have to ride on through the night under the stars looking for that place.

Maybe it was her emotional state after the day's events, but the music seemed to land right inside her heart. Something inside of her trembled like the chords of the guitar and the tears welled up in her eyes unbidden. She scooted back in the shadows of the house, hoping nobody would look at her and see her crying. But they were all focused on Wayne who played on, soothing them with his low voice. Every note was perfectly attuned to carry the feelings of the character he sang about.

Cade looped his arm around Lily who leaned into him with a tender smile on her face. One of the twins went to Gina who leaned down to brush her hair back. This was family. This was love. They had this place the cowboy longed for. They knew that what he ached for was theirs and they were grateful for it. They had each other on this special night.

Erin raised a hand to wipe her tears away. She didn't want to cry and attract attention, look weak or unhappy. She might be unhappy inside, maybe even the unhappiest person in the county after what had happened to her, but she need not show it. Mom had raised Livia and her to know that people with class and style hid their emotions. They never let themselves go. That was a sign of a lack of self-control. It was important to always show a calm face to the world even if inside you were angry or hurting. It would not do to demean yourself.

Those lessons taught when she was little had often helped her in life. To be strong and overcome difficulties or not lose her temper in an argument. She was grateful for it and she didn't blame her mother for what she had tried to instill in Livia and her. But here tonight those tears seemed natural and right, and still she blamed herself for them as if they were a sign of weakness. After all, Hutch had not been worth her love and attention. Why cry for him as if she missed him? As if losing him was a terrible thing. It was good she had seen him for what he was. A lousy traitor. It was good she had been saved the embarrassment of finding out later. She had not really lost anything. Just her fantasies of getting married and being happy. Fantasies they had been, because she knew deep down inside that she had never fully believed in Hutch and her. She had wanted to go through with the wedding to have what she dreamed of: someone to support her, someone to be there for her. But Hutch had only used her. He had never cared for her. Everything he had said had been a lie.

Wayne's song ended on a last drawn-out note. The night was still for a few heartbeats. She only heard the crackle of the coals on the barbeque and the chirping of a bird in the distance. Then Cade started to applaud. Lily looked up at him as if she thought it a little abrupt, maybe even inappropriate, but the others joined in. Gina called out to Wayne that he was fabulous and he had to play more songs. Wayne made a dismissive gesture but when Gina pleaded with him, he started to play some classics. The mood grew instantly light and the chatting resumed. The girls fetched a ball and threw it to each other. Rosie the border collie tried to join in, jumping up and knocking the ball away. There was laughter all around.

Erin sat quietly in the shadows, feeling a little robbed. The song had been so beautiful and fragile almost, touching her in a place inside where she was rarely emotional. Then it was over and everything seemed to be normal again, loud, boisterous, chaotic. That was how life was: one moment you watched the sunrise with your breath held because it was so pretty and the next you were caught in a thunderstorm and getting soaked to the skin by ice-cold rain. This was an ice-cold downpour kind of day and still Wayne's song had shown her a ray of light. Like a little golden lining along a dark stormy cloud.

"Are you okay?" April asked. She looked down on her with concern in her eyes. "You are sitting here all by yourself."

"It has been a long day. I was just thinking. But I'm glad I am here."

"And I'm glad to have you. You will soon see this place is fantastic. I mean, the town, the people. Everything about it." April came to sit by her side. Her expression was pensive. "You know, you might think I am singing its praises because I grew up here and this is my family's ranch, but I haven't always felt like it was the best place in the world. I have also cried while I lived here. It was…complicated after my father died and Cade took over and I felt like I wasn't welcome here. I was also in love with Matt, but he didn't see it and… It all seems so long ago, but I do remember how heartbroken I was. How it seemed like I would never be happy again. I do understand how you must be feeling right now. And I want you to know I am here for you if you want to talk or... For anything really. That is what friends are for."

"Thanks," Erin said. She couldn't get any more out without crying again. April called them friends, while they really didn't know each other all that well. She had thought of others as her friends, people who had let her down and deceived her. Everything seemed to have been turned upside down and she was dizzy from the ride. Part of her wanted to get away, to start walking and just keep on going to escape that sense of total failure. But she was too tired to walk far and besides, it was too late to run. People already knew and... She should make peace with the situation. Even if she didn't see how.

WAYNE PUT THE guitar away and looked to where he had left Erin. She was no longer there. He scanned the group and finally discovered her sitting in the shadows of the house. She looked even more dejected than earlier. How could he have thought that a little music could cheer her up? As if a simple song could repair the damage done to her heart.

Especially if the song came from him. *You are nothing special, son,* he could hear his father's voice say. *You think you are. You think that with your leather jacket and your guitar you can be a star. But you are just a country boy who will never make it in the music industry. Choose a profession that is stable and respectable.*

He had probably meant well. Wanted to save him from disappointment or shame. Dad was a practical man. Who wasn't into music at all. Didn't understand the beauty of it. How it enriched life.

Wayne fetched two glasses of lemonade and went over to Erin. He reached down to hand her a glass. "I want to propose a toast."

She looked up at him. Her eyes were a little shiny, as if she had been close to tears. It made his throat constrict. He didn't want to be funny now or distracting, he wanted to wrap an arm around her and tell her it was okay to cry because she was safe here.

"A toast?" she asked in an unsteady voice. She cleared her throat and continued, "What on earth for? It's not somebody's birthday, is it?"

"No. I just want to toast because life is good in its own way." He held his glass out to touch hers. "It can throw us curveballs all it likes, but when the day is done and we sit here together, we still have a lot to be grateful for. At least I know I have."

She considered this a moment. He saw the emotions flit across her face. Resentment at the idea there was anything to enjoy right now. But also acceptance because it was too late to change anything about the past. She couldn't keep fighting or running. It was time to surrender to the situation.

She touched her glass to his. "To life then. And to being grateful for what I still have." She hesitated and added with a careful smile, "Or what I have just discovered. Unexpected friends."

"Likewise." He raised the glass and as the cool liquid washed down his throat, he realized that he was really glad that he had met her, despite all the weird circumstances. That he felt like something connected them. And that he couldn't wait to see more of her when they started to work together for the anniversary celebrations.

CHAPTER SEVEN

ERIN AWOKE WITH a start thinking it was her wedding day and she was late. Late for the ceremony. The guests would be waiting. Her groom would be waiting. Where was her dress, the bouquet? She sat up in bed and swung her feet over the edge, already wondering how she could get ready in a short span of time. Then as her bare feet touched the ground, she realized she didn't recognize anything in the room as belonging to the resort where she was getting married. This was not her room. There was no dress hanging near the standing mirror. There was no suitcase in the corner. Where was she? What had happened?

Slowly it came back to her. Missing her hair comb, stepping out to ask Jenn for it… Seeing the horrible sight of her groom in the arms of her bridesmaid… The shock, the disbelief and at the same time the stomach-churning insight that she had always known deep inside that her relationship with Hutch would not last. That she wasn't pretty enough to satisfy him. That it was all her own fault because she had believed his lies and disregarded the doubts of family and friends. She had been ready to say *I do*, to commit for the rest of her life to a man who was not worth it. She could make nothing but bad decisions.

Erin hid her face in her hands and took a deep breath. She had to stop bashing herself. It had been Hutch's fault. He had not been faithful. He had used her. Lied to her, played around behind her back. He was to blame. She had to stay angry at him, instead of making herself smaller.

But truth be told, she felt so very, very small. How could she ever face her parents and Livia? Tell them it was over with Hutch and her. They would be glad but also say *told you so, he could not be trusted,* etc. She would look like the most naive person in the world for having believed Hutch's nice words. Only because she had so wanted to be loved.

She forced herself out of bed and onto the floor for push-ups. She had to exercise to feel better about herself. To show herself she had willpower and she could do things. By herself, for herself. It would be about her from now on. Her wants and needs. Not always catering to someone else's wishes. To what Hutch had wanted her to do, to wear, to cook, to buy for friends, to…

Livia had once said in anger that Erin was just like a parrot who only repeated other people's words. It had been an outburst uncharacteristic of her normally calm and controlled sister. She should not blame her for saying something hurtful that she had probably not really meant. Still, it echoed through her head now as she went through her morning routine of exercise, showering, dressing, brushing her teeth… She was a parrot. A copycat. Someone who mimicked other people's behavior and words, just because she had none of her own. No ambitions, no grand wishes.

She didn't have a five-year plan for her life. She could never answer the questions of *what is your biggest dream or your worst nightmare?* It was as if her mind blocked when she had to think like that. She did know what she liked and didn't like but…

And it was like, she realized now, not love. It was want, not need. Always a weaker version of what others displayed. She didn't feel the drive of the Olympian who settles for nothing but gold. Was she really that wishy-washy? So without zeal or purpose? So shallow and easy-going that she took everything for granted?

Where was the fire within that Dad always talked about? He had raised his daughters with a single goal in life: to be the number one in everything you did. Once you committed to something, you had to make it work. Not quit, not go back on your word, no, work for it, succeed. Livia had done all of that. She had made head cheerleader, she had been editor of the yearbook. She had graduated with straight As. She had excelled at gymnastics and tennis and…whatnot.

Sometimes Erin felt like her big sister had been turning everything she touched into gold. Oh, she had worked for it, trained for it, stayed up late for it. Erin would never say that it had come easy to Livia. But when she wanted something and went after it, it always worked out. With Erin it was never that way. She wanted something, a little, she gave it a try and it was kind of nice—or not—but she never had reached the point where it was all or nothing.

Well, maybe when she had chosen cruising over joining her parents' real estate firm. Then she had made up her mind and followed her own path. Much to their dismay.

And look what happened. You disappointed them. You let them down. You went to do something inferior. You wasted your talent. Then you met Hutch. You would never have met him if you hadn't gone into cruising. It was all because of that one fateful decision that your whole life unraveled. You made a crucial mistake by going against what your parents wanted for you. Perhaps even what was destined for you? It was all laid out on a silver platter and you rejected it because you thought you knew better. Now look how you've ended up.

Erin sighed as she stared at her reflection in the bathroom mirror. She had to get some breakfast in her stomach and focus on something other than the previous day. She had to look ahead and do work she liked just to relax her mind. She had to turn on her phone and wait for Wayne's call to pick her up to go into town and look at the venue for the anniversary celebrations. He had only wanted some tips, he had said. She could give him some. Valuable tips. There were things she was good at. She had to draw her confidence from there. And just forget about romance and wanting to find the one. Not everyone thrived in a relationship. Maybe being single was better for someone like her, who minded a lot what people said and who adjusted her ideas too easily to theirs. She could certainly save herself a lot of heartache by focusing on work.

WAYNE SAT IN his truck in the yard of the Carpenter Ranch Hotel as if he were sixteen and coming to call on the girl he was taking to the prom. He was not sure whether he was too early and Erin would be ready yet. Intruding now would make her feel uncomfortable and irritable and that was the last thing he wanted to do. He needed things to go smoothly today. If Erin decided once she had seen the venue and realized how much work it was that she didn't want to help, he was really in a jam. So he had to make sure she arrived in a good mood.

Yeah, sure. How to do that? Having just lost her fiancé the other day, how good could her mood be? He could not make it much better with jokes or light conversation. He was totally out of his depths here.

"Hey Wayne." Matt gestured at him through the front window.

Wayne felt rather sheepish as he exited the truck. "Hey. I uh…came to get Erin to go into town and have a look at the community center. She will do the floral decorations for the anniversary celebrations. At least I hope she will do them."

"I guess she will. I heard her and April talking about it last night." Matt smiled at him. "April can be quite a force when she has set her mind on something. And she thinks it's good for Erin to stay here for a while."

That was nice. An ally to help him make Erin feel better. Wayne cheered up a bit and asked, "Has Erin had breakfast yet?"

"I have no idea. I have been taking the baskets out to our guests." Matt gestured to the barn that had been redone to house several rooms for guests at his hotel. They booked a stay with breakfast included and all kinds of horse-related activities. Wayne wasn't sure whether Erin liked horses, she had only said something about pony rides as a kid, but he wanted to find out. He could take her out riding some time, to thank her for helping them out. She would of course also get paid, but an extra thank-you would be nice.

"Why don't you come in and you can see for yourself." Matt gestured him along. Carrying the empty baskets, he whistled a tune.

Wayne followed, dragging his feet. He felt a bit uneasy facing Erin again. The previous day it had been simpler because he hadn't known about her situation when she had popped up to ask for a ride, and later it had felt natural to help her along, but now in the light of a new morning, he realized how awkward her situation truly was and how bad she must feel about it. He felt a sort of shame of his own, as if by looking her in the eye, he'd make her relive the whole thing again and she'd be close to tears.

Matt led him past the reception area into the big family kitchen where breakfast was prepared for the guests and the family alike. April stood at the sink washing a pan probably used for eggs. An inviting scent was in the air: of omelets and toast, sausages and strawberry jam. Erin sat at the table, just finishing a glass of orange juice. Judging by the dirty plates and bowls at her place, she had at least not lost her appetite. That was good.

"Hi," he said smiling at her.

She put her glass down and wiped her mouth with a flush. "Good morning. I was just finishing breakfast."

"There is no rush," he said quickly. "Do have a cup of coffee or anything you like."

"Which probably means he wants coffee," Matt said reaching for the pot. "My mocha is famous."

Wayne wanted to protest but Matt had already handed him a mug of the most delicious-smelling coffee. He took a deep breath and then sipped. He closed his eyes and smiled in elation.

ERIN ALMOST HAD to laugh at Wayne's exaggerated expression of bliss. He could be truly funny. Now that he was around, she instantly felt better. She had a purpose for the day. She didn't have to sit around feeling miserable. No, they were going into town and she was going to dive into this whole celebration thing. With Wayne she could feel at ease because he was just supportive and kind like everyone around here was. She felt like she had come from a shark tank and suddenly landed in a quiet country brook where no one was after a piece of her. A nice break from reality. From the normal life she would have to get back to someday.

"What anniversary is it exactly?" she asked Wayne. He looked at her with a dazed expression. "Sorry?"

"The anniversary that you are celebrating. For which I will be decorating the community center."

"Oh, that. Heartmont's first homestead was built in this area exactly 150 years ago. A nice milestone. There have been preparations going on for quite a while. Banners made to hang in the streets, golden flags to go on lampposts, a whole schedule of events." Wayne put the mug away to pull out his phone. "I'll show you the website where it is all laid out." He scrolled a moment and then handed her the phone. His fingertips brushed her hand. The warmth of his touch seeped inside her as if the sun had come out on a gray day. "Have a look."

She leaned over the phone and angled it so there was no reflection on the screen. "Wow, this is a full program. A parade, concert, barbeque, orchard run..." She scanned all the events. "You have truly set it up in grand style."

"You know how it is in a community. Everybody wants to do something. Also to make sure that their ranch or business profits in some way by attracting tourists to them. These town celebrations are thought to bring in a lot of people who would normally just pass Heartmont to get to the Rockies."

"Oh, I see there is even an art competition. The best image of Heartmont will be selected by expert judges. All kinds of images are accepted: photographs, paintings, mixed media, videos. That sounds like fun."

"The local school is sending in drawings the kids made and I think a few elderly ladies are working on a large tapestry to present."

"Some farmer even cut the words *Heartmont 150* into his field and filmed it from on high with a drone." Matt leaned against the sink, sipping his own coffee. "Everyone is getting really creative."

"What are you doing?" Erin asked Wayne.

He blinked a moment. "Me? I'm helping out getting everything organized. Believe me, I have my hands full doing that."

"You could enter the competition." April eyed him. "You must have some image of Heartmont you could share. You grew up here. Maybe a collage of old photographs?"

Wayne's expression set. Erin could see his jaw tightening. She felt for him, realizing he was probably not eager to go back to the albums with photographs from his childhood. He had shared enough of his upbringing to make it clear to her that he had not been loved for who he was. His father had wanted to change him. That was always painful. She said quickly, looking at the phone, "And what on earth is a corn maze?"

"Have you never seen one?" April asked. "Or been inside one? They are great. You have to try it."

Matt explained that there were several in the area and the conversation floated from one event to another, letting Wayne gently off the hook. From the corner of her eye Erin saw him relax again. He wore a checkered shirt today, faded blue jeans and cowboy boots with elaborate stitching. He was freshly shaven and even his hair was still a little damp, combed back neatly. It looked like he had spruced himself up for the occasion. She got up to get her things so they could be on their way. Wayne took her outside and pointed at his truck. "I hosed her down this morning. There really was mud all over her."

"Her? Is it a she?"

"I guess so." He shrugged, uncomfortably. "I never called a car anything else but her. I take good care of her."

"Does she also have a name?"

"No. But I call her names when she won't start. I do the same with my tractor and any other thing that refuses to cooperate."

"Just with things or also with people?" she asked with a wink as she got into the truck. He closed the door for her and rounded the vehicle to get in on his side. She thought he would leave her question hanging, but once he was in the seat, pulling the seat belt across his chest, he looked her in the eye and said, "I am usually very patient with people. Just not with equipment that fails me. If it's a computer thing, it's even worse."

"You get ready to throw the thing out of a window?" she asked with a smile.

"Something like that. I can't help myself." He started the engine. The radio came on. It was some local station with what her father would call hillbilly music. It was odd how trained her mind was to detect things her parents would not like. Perhaps she had even gone cruising to be able to have a life away from them and their opinions. But even on the cruises she had kept doing things they enjoyed. Like all those classical concerts she had been reminded of last night. Why had she not also gone to see local dancing or to a small bar where a spoken word poet performed? Why had she not tried new things, but instead fallen into the same old beaten track again?

She kneaded her hands. He glanced at her. "How are you with computers? Always getting them to do what you want?"

"Basically, yes, I can't recall the last time they really turned rebellious on me."

"A good leader." He grinned. "I like that." He turned the radio off. In the sudden silence she could hear the tinkling of the little silver horse charm on his rearview mirror.

"Is that for good luck?" she asked, pointing at it.

"No, I don't believe in luck. Not in the sense that you can influence it by charms and stuff." He was silent a moment, staring at the road as if he considered whether he wanted to tell her the story or not. Then he said, "My mother used to wear that on a necklace. I remember that it caught the sunlight when she leaned down over me. I was very small so I don't recall much else. But that one memory is very vivid. I got the charm after she died. That is… I took it. It was in her room, in the little box on her dressing table and I sneaked in and I took it. I don't know if my father ever knew I had it. Or that he even thought to look for it. Maybe not. He was different after she passed away. He avoided mentioning her. Sometimes it was as if…she had never even existed."

Wayne clenched the wheel. The tightness in his hands seemed to make Erin's stomach feel tense. As if his pain transferred to her.

He said, "I wanted to have something of her. Something to hold onto. I always kept that. And once I had my own life and my own house and truck I hung it on that mirror so I see it a lot. I look at it and I…" He fell silent. His jaw worked hard as if he had to keep himself from tearing up.

Erin was sorry she had asked about it. She didn't know what to say. Actually, she just wanted to reach out and put her hand on his. But he was driving.

Besides, she hardly knew him so that would be weird. But still…it was so difficult to watch him struggle. To realize he had never been allowed to grieve. That little kid inside of him still felt a deep pain over the loss of his mother.

WAYNE DIDN'T KNOW why he even told her this. He could have simply lied that it was indeed a good luck charm or invented some story about where he had gotten it. But he felt it was important to be honest with Erin. She had been lied to enough. By too many people. People she had cared for who had let her down.

Now, he might just be a stranger, but he intended to be honest with her. Always. Even when it hurt. Like it did now.

To know his father hadn't wanted them to say a word about their mom. That he and Alex hadn't been allowed to cry even because they had to be big boys. Maybe it had been hard for Dad to see their tears and not know what to say but could he not just have hugged them? Comforted them without words by his presence? He had still been there even if Mom hadn't. But Dad had kept them at arm's length. It had hurt.

At least Wayne had hurt. Maybe not Alex. He had never said so at least. His life was successful. Everything seemed to be going his way. He had found a lovely wife, had kids. It was like he had followed the route that most people did: build a career, start a family, settle down. Now Wayne was also settled, sort of, in the sense that he had a house, work, an income from his ranching and dog breeding. He wasn't doing all that bad, he supposed. But sometimes it felt like he had missed out and others had done much better. They had at least adhered to the common ideal of marrying and family.

Erin said, "I hope I didn't ruin your day asking about it."

He glanced at her. She gave him an honest stare that cut right to his core. He couldn't shrug this off with a grin or some goofy remark like he usually did when people came too close. He looked ahead again. "My day is not that easily ruined. You know, it's…been a long time since I was that little boy."

"But still you keep the charm here in the truck." She touched it gingerly with her index finger. "You want to keep your mother close."

A warm feeling seeped through him. Not pain but…joy in a strange sort of way. Yes, he wanted to keep her close and she was close and Erin understood that. She simply understood that without him having tried to tell her.

Erin said, “I guess you must think I’m a pretty harsh person to have kept my own parents away from my wedding. That I don’t love them at all or I wouldn’t have done that.”

“I don’t judge easily. Especially not when I don’t know anything about the situation. You must have had your reasons. Besides, maybe you just wanted to get married with nobody else present. People do that.”

“I guess so. But the thing is, Hutch’s entire family was present. All of his friends. It was all focused on him, on what he liked and wanted. Nobody asked me. I guess I could have tried to influence things more but… I felt sort of trapped in all of the arrangements. It happened without me really noticing what was going on until it was too late.”

“It was not too late because you got away.” He felt relief wash through him at this conclusion. She had gotten away from that man who had wanted to own her. Who had thought he could use Erin for his own purposes. And then discard her? What had been his plans?

Anger rushed through his veins and he hoped he would never come face-to-face with this guy. He'd be tempted to give him a piece of his mind.

Erin said, "It's strange when I look back on it how I got caught up in the whirl of having been chosen by this wonderful man and… It was like a movie script you know. We met on a skiing trip, we frolicked in the snow, we kissed and…it all seemed perfect. I was like Cinderella at the ball. Out of my depths but totally happy with my prince."

"And then?" he asked. He didn't want to look at her now so he didn't have to see whether she was pining for the guy. It could be. He had hurt her, but she might still miss him. Life was weird that way.

Erin sighed. "I guess there was the stroke of twelve at midnight. And everything turned back to what it had been before. I wasn't a princess after all."

"Or he was never a prince but a frog."

Erin had to laugh. The sound cheered him up a little. She could still laugh.

She shook her head. "That's another fairy tale, Wayne." She sobered and added, "But thanks anyway. You do make me feel a little bit better." She was thoughtful for a moment.

"I am so glad you happened to be at the resort. It was almost like…it was meant to be. I mean you brought me to Heartmont, to April, and… now I can also help with the anniversary celebrations. It gives me a legit reason to be here."

"Do you need one?" he asked, a little taken aback by her word choice. Who would be checking on her to see where she was and what she was doing?

Erin flushed. She fumbled with her hands. "I turned my phone back on this morning and I just thought that maybe…my mother would call as she does every now and then, or Livia, my sister, and I could uh…you know, casually tell them I am working and… I…feel bad about shutting them out. They don't know, which is all the better, but I still feel like I have to answer to them for what I did."

"They don't know about the wedding," he concluded. "So they also don't know about this guy's behavior to you and how you ran. But won't they find out it's over between the two of you?"

"Eventually yes, but I hope to postpone that a little. They won't ask about Hutch as they never approved of him, so I don't have to lie like we are still together." Erin sighed. "I am not up to explanations right now. I would just break apart and they'd tell me he's not worthy of my tears and heartache. Like I don't know that."

"Do you still care for him?" Wayne asked. He didn't know why he did, but he felt he had to.

Erin looked at him. Her eyes were wide and questioning. "He betrayed me with one of my friends. Why would I still care? I should hate him."

"You say, should hate him, not do hate him."

Erin turned her head to gaze out of the side window. Her expression was sad and he just wanted to tell her to cheer up and it would all be better soon. But that would sound awfully shallow. She said slowly, "I don't know how I feel. Part of me doesn't want to let go of the hopes and dreams I had for my wedding and married life. It seemed so wonderful. Like I would finally belong. But then again part of me also knows that I was never safe with Hutch. I always had to perform to be good enough for him."

"So it is a good thing it ended." He said it thoughtfully, without feeling glad about it. "For you. It's not right to try and change yourself. You are okay the way you are."

"That is a line from every self-help book in

the world." She sounded angry now, ready to jump at him.

"That's funny because I have never read a self-help book in my life."

"It's a total cliché. If we are all good the way we are, then why are we constantly trying to change ourselves? New clothes, new hairdo, new habits. New Year's resolutions. Everybody knows that's true."

"I guess it's fun to try new things. To reinvent yourself once in a while. Or just stretch yourself and get out of your comfort zone. But you cannot and should not change the essence of yourself. The things that make you you."

"I guess I have done so much adjusting in the past few months I have almost forgotten who I am. In any case I don't know what I want." Erin said it in a low voice. "Or what I should want. Maybe I did everything wrong. I mean, even before I was with Hutch. Mom and Dad always wanted me to go into their business. In real estate. I was good at it too, I mean, helping to refurnish apartments and condos and vacation homes to sell them to the highest bidder. I loved staging the properties following all the interior decorating trends. I often spent Saturdays going to museums and looking at art for inspiration. I didn't necessarily love all the high-end parties that went with it to meet and greet clients, that's more Mom and Dad's end of things, but I loved the creativity that went into making a place look its best for potential buyers. I flew all around the country to meet people which got me more interested in traveling. I focused more and more on flowers and plants and… I guess I could get back into the company doing that."

"Don't you want to go cruising again? Having met the wrong man doesn't mean you have to quit your job."

"I guess cruising was just a way to escape my responsibilities in the company. I mean, family is important in life. It gives stability. And there were aspects to my work in the company I really liked. City life always fit me like a glove. When I just think about all the things you can do, from dawn to dusk… On the cruise ship we had our own world with entertainment and fine food, but I was a worker there, not a holiday maker. I did miss those impulse decisions of going to see a movie and then having pizza at some place. The buzz of things."

A true city girl, he thought. Heartmont had remarkably little buzz by that measure.

"I feel tired now, like I've been on the run for years," Erin said. "Just running to get away.

It could be time to just look over my shoulder and face what I have been running away from."

They were at the edge of the town and Wayne steered the truck down the street then to the right into the parking lot. He turned off the engine and looked at Erin. She sat there huddled like a little bird in a storm. He felt so sorry for her but didn't want to say so. She didn't need someone to make her feel smaller and less adequate but to build her up and boost her confidence. Even if that would take her away from here and back into the life she had once left behind. "Take this time here as a time-out. To do a reevaluation of everything. The outcome may surprise you."

She looked up at him, a question mark in her beautiful eyes. "Why do you say that?"

"Because I am a terrific judge of character and I just know that you have a lot more going for you than you give yourself credit for."

Erin flushed and at the same time a smile crept around her lips. "Thanks, Wayne, it's sweet of you to say so."

"I mean it," he insisted and then opened the car door. "Let's go see the community center." After she got out and he had locked the truck, they walked to the big building that formed the heart of the town and of their community life. At the double glass doors leading inside he halted and looked back. “I brought a box with printed posters to distribute around town to promote all the anniversary events. I’d better go back and get it. You go inside and wait for me in the room immediately to your right.”

He walked back quickly across the lot and got the box out of the back of his car. Carrying it on his arm, he returned to the entrance. From the other side of the street a woman crossed to the center. She was tall and carried herself with a certain self-important air. Her smart business suit could very well be tailor-made and her high heels probably came from a luxury brand. Just like her leather shoulder purse. She seemed totally out of place in a little town like Heartmont. Her cool gaze descended on him and she slowed her pace. “Excuse me, do you work here?”

“Uh, yes, at the moment,” he said, glancing up and down at her attire. Was she involved with some development company that had laid eyes on land around town? They had dealt with several such situations through the years and the idea that new vultures had descended just filled his stomach with ice.

The woman said, “Good. I am looking for someone and I hoped you might be able to help here at this community center. To get a list of all hotels and B&Bs so I can check in to see where they are staying." Her tone was determined, bordering on grim. "It's really important I get in touch with them about an important matter."

Wayne said, "Oh, I see. Can't you just call them? I suppose you do have a phone number?"

"I do, but the situation requires a face-to-face meeting. It is not news I can share over the phone."

That sounded serious. "I do know most people around here so I might be able to help you find the persons you need," he offered.

"They are from out of town. Only holidaying here. Or should I say honeymooning?" The tone was ice-cold now. "Mr. and Mrs. Hutch Michaels."

Hutch was the name of Erin's treacherous fiancé. Wayne felt a surge of energy through his system. "And you are?" he inquired casually.

"Livia Lakewood. Sister of the bride."

CHAPTER EIGHT

WAYNE COULD JUST prevent himself from dropping the box with the posters right in front of her feet. Erin had made it very clear that she wasn't eager for her family to find out about her situation. Now her sister was here. In the flesh. Standing right before him. She didn't know that the wedding had not taken place. She assumed Erin had married Hutch and they were now happily enjoying their honeymoon here. What news did Livia come with? News she wanted to deliver in person…

"Could you give me such a list of hotels and B&Bs?" she asked, hitching a perfectly formed brow. He had to be staring at her like a fish out of water.

"Why don't you, uh…" He had to find some way to keep Livia away from Erin. So she couldn't go inside here. He had to direct her to some other place in town. But what place? "Try the general store. Mrs. Jones is a gold mine of information. If a couple of newlyweds are staying around town, she will certainly know about it."

Livia Lakewood gave him a suspicious look. "Are you sure? It seems far more likely I should start my quest right here. This is like a town hall, isn't it? I am not familiar with how small towns work, but this looks like an official building. I don't have all day."

"The general store is much better..." Wayne tried vaguely.

Livia snorted. "I am sorry, mister, but I am not after gossip, but after factual information. I will just ask inside. Sorry to have bothered you." She strode past him on her high heels and entered the building. Wayne rushed after her. He could just catch the closing door with his free hand. He scanned the entrance hall for Erin. If she had listened to him and gone into the room to the right, she was safe. He supposed. Livia Lakewood would go to the reception desk on the left to ask her question.

But there was no one at the reception desk and after a quick glance across it and to the staircase beyond, Livia turned her attention to the door on the right. With determined strides she went for it.

"Not in there," he called, desperate for

some excuse to keep her away from that room. "There is a drama performance..."

But she had already opened the door and gone inside. Wayne followed in a rush. His heart was pounding and he physically tensed all over at the idea of the confrontation that was about to come.

ERIN TURNED WHEN the door opened. That had to be Wayne with his posters. She was glad that he had hurried back because she had a lot of questions about the project. She couldn't wait to get started on something that would take her thoughts off her situation.

But it wasn't Wayne's tall cowboy figure filling the doorway. It was a female silhouette, crisp and perfect. And when the woman closed in on her, Erin felt her jaw go slack. "Livia..." she breathed, just as Livia cried out, "Erin!"

They stood staring at each other a few feet apart, both unable to get anything else out. Erin could only think *oh no, oh no this should not have happened. What is she doing here? Why did she come?*

Livia regained her composure first. She straightened up like she always did when she wanted to gain ground in a conversation and said, "Hello, Erin. Or should I say Mrs. Michaels?" She reached out a hand with a perfect French manicure. "Congratulations on your wedding."

Erin didn't take the hand. She was too stunned. Livia knew she had been getting married. Did Mom and Dad also know? Were they around? Could they come in any minute? Would Mom ask her why, would Dad just look utterly disappointed in her? She felt more miserable by the second and wanted to crawl into some closet to get away.

Livia said, "I am sure it was a beautiful day. That you had everything you wanted. A gorgeous venue, a cake with layers, a stunning dress and a huge party with all of your friends. It must have been fantastic. A little over-the-top maybe. Judging by the costs."

Erin blinked. Livia was totally losing her. She didn't understand how Livia had found out about the wedding. How she had known to come here to confront her. Or why she even thought there had been a wedding since Erin had run away. It was so confusing.

Livia said, "Look, Erin, I know you never liked our criticism of Hutch. And maybe we were wrong to say he wasn't right for you. Maybe you felt like we never gave him a chance and it only made you all the more determined to push on with this relationship. I am sure that we made our mistakes." She spoke in a collected tone but Erin saw by the color rising in her neck and cheeks that Livia was getting worked up. Emotional almost. "But you had no right to do this," she went on. "To cut Mom and Dad out of your wedding day and then send the bill to the firm."

Erin was too stunned to respond. Hutch had pressed her to pick up the bills for the wedding, yes, but there had been an agreement to send those to her personally. She had filled out her contact information, not her parents'. How had the manager at the resort gotten his hands on the email address of the firm?

Livia continued, "To let them pay for everything that you enjoyed without even letting them know you were getting married. It was a good thing that I opened the email. Mom would have been devastated. Not to mention how Dad would have reacted. Do you want to hurt them somehow? What did they do wrong? They didn't agree with your choices, but...they are still your parents."

"I never denied that," Erin said. Her voice sounded thin and breakable. She wished she could be firm now and show Livia what she was made of but she just wanted to hide. She didn't know where to start first with the explanations. "I didn't invite any of you because..."

"That doesn't matter," Livia said cutting her off. "You have a right to marry without us present. I doubt I would have wanted to come anyway. Knowing how I feel about Mr. Michaels. But to send the bill to Mom and Dad, that is really a low blow. I can't see why you would want to hurt them that way. I just had to come and ask you. I called the resort mentioned on the bill and some young girl who answered the phone said that the wedding party had left and the only thing she had overheard was the mention of the town of Heartmont. Some friend of yours from cruising having a hotel there?"

Erin's heart hammered in her chest. Hutch had discussed her possible whereabouts. Had Jenn offered the information that a former colleague had a hotel here? She also knew April from stints on the ship. But no one had shown up at the ranch hotel. So they didn't want to get in touch with her. They had probably merely laughed at the idea of her running to hide with someone she knew. "She didn't know a name for the hotel or the friend," Livia continued. "Which induced me to come here to this official building to find more information. I mean, how many hotels can a small town like this have? And with people probably knowing everything about each other I figured I could find out which hotel is managed by someone who worked in cruising. Of course I could also just have tried to call you but I wasn't about to have you hang up on me. I wanted to have this conversation face-to-face. I am glad I caught you without your husband. I am sure he would have an answer for everything. But he is not family. You are. I want to hear it straight from you. What is this low blow with the bill being sent to Mom and Dad?"

Erin blinked. Her brain refused to process any of this. The bill was not supposed to have gone to Mom and Dad. How had the resort found out about the company email? It made no sense. "I don't understand what you are saying."

Livia snorted. "It is not that hard to understand is it, dear Erin? You got married at our parents' expense."

"No." Erin shook her head. Livia was just wrong here and she wasn't about to take the blame for something she hadn't done. After all the mistakes she had made, she hadn't done this one thing Livia was now accusing her of. "I didn't send them any bill. I didn't ask the resort to send them the bill either. I paid a deposit in advance and we agreed that the detailed bill would be send to *my* email address on the wedding day. I never provided their email address."

"Yes you did." Livia was now red as a tomato. "You even have the nerve to deny it? How could you. There is proof. Here it is." She pulled up her phone and thrust it at Erin. "Look at the email. Then tell me whether you sent it or not. Don't give me these lousy excuses..."

Erin accepted the phone with shaking hands. She had to focus not to drop it and damage Livia's expensive property. She stared at the screen. There it was, a list of items, prices... The venue, the pre-wedding day dinner, the party... All billed to Lakewood Real Estate. What?

She looked up at Livia. Her lips were trembling. How could she even say anything to make this better? The only conclusion possible was that Hutch had provided the company email address to deal her this extra blow. He could have easily found it on the company website and then claimed to the resort manager that the family of the bride was picking up the tab anyway. Because they had enough money. She could just hear him say it.

Livia frowned. Her eyes flashed in a moment

of confusion. "You…look as if you didn't know. As if you are seeing this for the first time."

"I am." Erin wet her lips and handed back the phone. "I have nothing to do with this email. I can only imagine that Hutch did it. But I didn't know."

"Oh." Livia stood motionless. Her high color faded a little and she seemed to search for words. For an apology even?

But then her stance straightened anew. "You may not have sent it, but you did marry the jerk who did. I can't forgive you for that. You never wanted to see what type of man he really is. A liar and a cheat who is only marrying you for your family's money. This—" she waved the phone "—is the proof. At last. But it is too late now, isn't it? You married him. You are *his* wife."

"I am sorry…" a male voice said.

Erin jerked upright at the idea that Wayne had witnessed this painful situation. He stood there holding a cardboard box. He looked at Livia and shook his head slowly. "You are understandably upset but you don't give Erin half a chance to explain."

Livia glowered at him. "You? I asked you outside the building where I might find Mr. and Mrs. Michaels. You knew I meant Erin, didn't you? That she was in here. And you tried to steer me away by making up this story about the general store being the HQ of town gossip. What kind of conspiracy is this? Is the entire town in league with you and Hutch, to hide you from us?"

Wayne said quietly, "I'm sorry that I lied to you. I just wanted Erin to have some time to know that you were here and…"

"Prepare her story," Livia huffed. "I don't want a made-up tale full of convenient lies. I want the truth."

"The truth," Erin said. It was like she came to life suddenly. As if that dreadful stillness inside of her broke and she knew what to say. "The truth is that Hutch and I didn't marry. I saw the light that he was using me and I ran away before we could tie the knot. I left him, Livia. That must have made him so mad he billed the whole thing to Mom and Dad. He must have thought they somehow talked me into leaving."

Livia blinked. Her complexion was pale now and her eyes full of confusion. "Sorry? You didn't marry him?"

Erin shook her head. "The wedding didn't take place. I walked away from it all."

Livia stood there staring at her. She seemed to be at a loss for words.

For once.

Usually Livia had an answer to everything.

Then she walked over, threw her arms around Erin and hugged her tightly. "Oh Erin. You finally came to your senses. You realized that you were about to throw away your entire life on that loser. I am so so glad. You did the right thing and now… Mom and Dad will be so happy too. They will want to see you."

Erin stood rigidly. Livia's hug felt like she was forced back into the cage from which she had escaped. *Good, you did what we wanted, now you can come back to do what we wanted all along.* This wasn't what Erin had intended at all.

Livia released her and held her by the shoulders. "I am so proud of you. You have more sense than I gave you credit for. I thought you were blinded by your love for him. But you caught wind of what he was up to and… You left him standing at the altar. It must have hurt his ego badly. So he decided to send the bill to us. As a final blow. Such a pathetic vengeful little thing to do. It does shine even more light on his true character. I'm so glad you broke up with him. I'll even gladly pay the expenses. Just to be rid of him."

"No, you won't." Erin said it calmly. Livia's glee felt so unwarranted. She had not stood up Hutch to hurt him. Or to prove her parents right. And they need not pay for a reception they had never wanted to take place. A party they would never have attended. "There wasn't a wedding or a party so Hutch cannot bill for that. I did realize earlier there were preparations made and I will have to cover the pre-wedding dinner and the cancellation fee. Maybe we can split the bills as we both prepared for the wedding believing it would take place." Livia didn't need to know Hutch had betrayed her. In light of that Erin could not be expected to pay for everything alone? "I will look into it. And yes, if I have to, I will get legal counsel. I am old enough to arrange my own affairs."

Livia stepped back. A chill invaded her voice. "I see. I am not needed here. Well, all the better that Mom and Dad don't know a thing. You take care of it then and...get in touch later. Mom does want to hear from you. It means a lot to her." Livia hesitated another moment as if she wanted to say more, then she turned away. Her heels clicked on the floor as she made for the door. She didn't acknowledge Wayne, not even with a brief nod.

As soon as the door closed behind her sister, Erin felt like melting into the floorboards. Her knees were jelly and she could hardly breathe. This was such a humiliation. She had been forced to admit to Livia that she had canceled her wedding to Hutch. Livia admired her for it, not knowing she had just run in shame because Hutch had been two-timing her. How could she ever face Livia again? Or her parents?

Wayne came over to her. He put the cardboard box on a table and asked, "Are you okay?"

"No, I am not. That seems logical, right? And what did you mean, lying to her like that?"

"She asked me for a way to get a list of hotels and B&Bs because she was looking for Mr. and Mrs. Michaels. I could hardly tell her there was no such couple. That wasn't for me to do. I just wanted her to go someplace else so I could inform you that she was here and you had time to think up a way to..."

"Yes, sure." Erin waved him off. She sank onto a chair. "I should have known Livia would somehow find out. She always finds out about things I do wrong so she can come and rub them in my face. That is what big sisters do, right?"

"She did seem happy the wedding didn't take place. She must have thought you were about to make a mistake that could hurt you."

"Hurt them. Hurt the family name. Business. Cost money, whatever." Erin gestured wildly. "That is how they think. It was never about me. They just didn't want me to bring shame to them. Or financial ruin." She clenched her hands. "I feel so bad about this. That this is the way they found out about the whole disaster."

"Livia seems to think you came to your senses and said no to this man she never liked. That does make it better in her book."

"Oh, wonderful. Should I be happy now that my sister at least doesn't totally hate me? She thinks I made the decision to leave."

"Didn't you?"

Erin shook her head without speaking. Tears burned her eyes. She had been forced to break things off with Hutch, forced by the sight of him kissing Jenn, forced by the hurtful words she had overheard. That had broken her so much she had run away like a crying child. It had not been a decision, let alone one made with her head held high. With confidence or self-esteem.

Wayne said, "You did make a decision. You packed up and left."

"I ran. That's different. I got a shock and I turned away and I ran. Because it was just impossible to stay. That is not a choice." She clenched her hands so tightly her nails cut into her flesh. "Hutch made the choice for me by betraying me. Jenn made the choice for me by saying hurtful things about me. I was so humiliated I couldn't stay."

"But you would have wanted to stay? Marry this man you never felt safe with?"

Erin knew Wayne was right but she didn't want to admit it. His insistence just made her angry. It was as if all the tension she'd felt when Livia was here, accusing her, now burst out.

"I didn't tell you stuff to have it flung back at me. You don't know a thing about my life, what I think, want or how I should decide. Just go away and leave me. I want to be alone now. Just go."

Wayne stood a moment, wavering. She saw it in his stance as he started forward as if to confront her. Or maybe just wrap her in a hug? She badly needed one. Just a friendly hug to tell her everything was alright.

He moved back. "Okay," he said in a hoarse voice. "I'll go away then." He turned and walked to the door. As his hand fell on the knob, he stalled. "You be careful. Don't do anything rash while you are mad and hurt."

She watched as he opened the door wider. She didn't really want him to go away. She didn't want to be alone. In the silence and the emptiness she would just feel all the more how everything she had ever done in her life had been wrong. How she was a total failure.

"Wayne..." Her voice almost cracked. "I am sorry. Don't go away. Just don't...leave me."

WAYNE STOOD WITH his back to her. He understood how she felt, that she just had to lash out at someone to vent. That someone happened to be him because he was present, on the scene.

But still it hurt. It was hardly his fault that her sister had turned up and had been upset about the bill being sent to their parents. It had been a nasty trick by Hutch, a final blow when he had already hurt Erin so much. But why did she have to take out her pain on him?

"Please..." Erin's voice was soft and lined with tears. "Don't go. I am sorry."

Wayne turned to her. He didn't close the distance, yet. He feared he might do something inappropriate like hold her in his arms. He so wanted to take her pain away and make her feel better. But he had to be careful. She was vulnerable and he shouldn't take advantage of the situation.

"I am so sorry." Erin's face contorted and tears streamed down her cheeks. "I am just doing everything wrong. But when Livia said how happy she was that it was over and she hugged me, it felt like...another betrayal. Now I can come back and be what they want me to be, but...she is not sorry for me that I lost the man I thought I loved. That I lost all I believed in. Wanted to believe in, in any case."

"That must be hard for her to grasp right now." Wayne closed the distance slowly. Her tears made it even more difficult for him not to reach out and touch her. Brush them away, tell her it would be alright again. If she just gave it a little time.

"Your sister is a very strong personality, I bet. She doesn't let her feelings show easily. She came here all worked up about an injustice. She was then confronted with a completely different scenario. For a moment her guard slipped and she showed you how happy she was that you didn't marry this man she thought bad for you. I think that was genuine emotion on her part."

"You are actually taking Livia's side?" Erin sounded disbelieving and hurt.

Wayne lifted up his hands, palms out to appease her anger. "I just want you to think about it for a second. She felt relieved that you escaped a bad marriage. Doesn't that mean she cares for you?"

"Maybe." Erin sighed and slumped in the chair again. "I just wish she hadn't come here. I felt safe here. Hidden away from the world. Now she is here in my hiding place and…"

"You told her the truth. That is out of the way." Wayne came to stand close to her. He smiled down on her. "You have done something you didn't think you could do."

"Yeah, because I was forced to do it after she tracked me down and confronted me. It wasn't a choice, just like leaving the resort wasn't a choice either. I am always reacting to things, I am never acting myself. I just wish I was different. Better somehow."

"You are…"

"If you are going to say perfect the way you are, I am going to kick you." Erin came to her feet. "Look, I know we came here to talk about flowers and all, but I need to do something else first. I want to go back to the resort and talk to the manager there about the bill for the party. I understand that preparations were made and we did have the pre-wedding dinner but…

maybe, under the circumstances, I won't have to pay the full amount? I want to discuss the situation with him. It is rather unusual I suppose, and I want to know what my options are. I need to…act, you know."

Wayne nodded. "Alright. I will drive you out there. I know the manager and maybe I can uh…help you smooth things over?"

Erin hesitated a moment. She didn't want his help to clean up her mess. She felt bad enough about everything. But it was a good idea to have someone present who knew the manager and might wield some influence. If they could do something about the bill, get Hutch to cover part of it somehow, that would be wonderful.

She needed Wayne to go with her. She needed him to… Not only to help her as a local contact but also as a friend. To be there beside her when she had to face her difficulties, head-on.

CHAPTER NINE

WHEN THEY ARRIVED at the resort and asked for the manager, they were told he was busy right now but they could wait in his office. They were guided there and invited to sit on the chairs in front of his desk until he came.

Erin felt like the chair was burning as she sat there, nervously twiddling with her hands. This was even worse than waiting for a job interview or having to see the principal in school. She recalled how their high school principal had always made sure that when a student was called in, he or she had to sit there alone in the office for a while. That waiting was the worst. Not knowing what would come next.

Wayne gently touched her arm. “It will be alright. There is always a solution for every situation. If you talk it over.”

“Easy for you to say. It’s not your wedding that went wrong and your bills that are outstanding.”

"No, but I have been in a position where I had bills to pay and no money to pay them. I know how it feels when you think your entire life is on the line."

She looked at his face, at the tight lines around his lips, the shadow of tiredness under his eyes. It was like she could suddenly see that he wasn't just a tough cowboy who took care of himself, but also a man who carried responsibility for his ranch, his animals, his land and the community. A man who also took that responsibility very seriously. Someone to depend on.

The door opened and the manager came in. He greeted Wayne, hurried to sit behind his desk and rifled through some papers. "I have a very full schedule today. What can I do for you?"

"It's about the bill for the party. The wedding party?" Erin wet her lips. "I do understand that costs were incurred but…the actual party didn't take place so…"

The man looked at her with cold blue eyes. "The actual party did take place. Exactly as planned. There was a cake, a reception, dinner and dancing. With all of the guests who stayed here. The full arrangement." He waited a moment before adding, "Except for the actual wedding ceremony, so you will not have to pay for that."

Erin stared at him. She opened her mouth to say something but nothing came out. Hutch and his family and friends had actually celebrated the wedding, but without the wedding having taken place? They had partied, but without a bride? How strange was that. How cruel. Like it was just about Hutch and them and it didn't matter whether she had been there or not.

It probably didn't.

The manager said, "I had originally taken down your contact information to send the bill to, but I was told to now send the bill to your family's real estate firm to ensure the costs would be covered. I checked the website and your photo was on there as an employee."

Erin cringed. When she had left the firm to work on the cruise ship, her parents had seen it as a temporary thing, a sort of belated teen rebellion. They had not removed her profile from the company website to pretend to outsiders that she still worked there.

"Is there a problem?" the manager asked with narrowed eyes. "When we are not paid promptly, we use a payment service to ensure that we get the money we are entitled to."

Meaning there was no point pleading with

him because he wanted his money. Which was probably understandable from his point of view. It was not his problem that Hutch and his family had decided to get back at her.

Wayne said, "Look, Roy, this is a situation you have never had before, I imagine. The bride leaves the wedding venue, there is no actual wedding, but still you are told that the festivities will go on. You must have realized it was awkward."

"Of course, but...the people were already staying here, the cake had been delivered, dinner was being prepared and... I told the groom that if we canceled the whole thing, there would still be considerable costs to be paid. The situation of cancellation, even on the day itself, is covered in the contract. So he said they might as well go through with it. His family and friends had traveled a long way, to be there, had bought clothes and... Well, he also wanted them to have a good time in spite of it all."

"Then he should pay for this good time," Erin said. Her voice trembled with anger. "I don't mind that they had a party without me but my family is not paying for that."

The manager leaned back in his chair. "I just mentioned that if you had canceled the whole thing, there would also have been costs. You cannot simply walk away from something that big."

"I do understand. But I already paid a substantial deposit. Hutch caused our breach. He can hardly expect me to pick up the pieces."

Wayne said, "Roy, look, we can work something out..."

The manager raised his hands and cut across him, "Wayne, I do appreciate all you do for the resort. You have always been a good friend and neighbor to me but this is business. People come here, a whole group of them, they rent rooms and organize a wedding party and... I can't simply say look, forget about paying for it. I don't run a charity here. I have staff who need to be paid. Local business people deliver items like cake, flowers. I can't tell them that they won't be paid. I just need to ensure that we are all paid for services rendered."

Wayne leaned forward and repeated, "We can work something out..."

The manager stood up. "I can't help you. If you feel that something went wrong here, you must find legal counsel. They can advise you about your position and tell you what to do to set things right. I can't make those decisions. I am sorry." He walked to the door and turned back to say to Wayne, "I am really sorry. But that is the way it is." He left the room and closed the door.

Wayne huffed. "That went well. I guess I hoped I would have more influence with him."

"I understand his position." Erin sat there with shoulders slumped, dejection filling her. "My problems, Hutch's betrayal and my response to it, are not his to solve. He simply wants his money. I will just have to…find a way to sort out who has to pay him." She took a deep breath. "I feel miserable at the idea of going to a lawyer. I don't want anyone to know and now I have to constantly let people in on it because I can't sort it out otherwise." She buried her face in her hands. "I am almost tempted to just pay the bills and be done with it."

Wayne was silent a moment. Then he said, "I do know a lawyer who might be able to help you. We could go and see him. I mean, I could also call him myself and explain the situation and ask if he can help. You can just focus on getting a flower display ready for the community center."

Erin lowered her hands and stared at Wayne. "You would do that? Take care of this mess for me? Why?"

"Because you are helping me with the anniversary preparations. That makes us even.

I mean, you will probably be paid by the anniversary committee for the time invested in working with the flowers, but…that you want to help out, while you are going through such a hard time, means enough to me to want to help you with your troubles. Okay?"

Wayne held Erin's gaze as he waited for her reaction. He had expected her to jump at the chance of getting legal advice, but she seemed reluctant. Maybe he had misjudged the depth of their bond. He had simply picked her up at the resort and taken her into town to find a place to stay. He wasn't a close friend or anything.

Erin took a deep breath and then she suddenly leaned forward and gave him a hug. It was a very brief embrace, almost as if she didn't trust herself to really do it. But it felt good to feel her touch, her warmth close to him. It confirmed to him that he was doing the right thing here, even if he felt like he didn't know what he was doing at all.

"Thanks, you are a real friend," she said in a hoarse voice. "I wonder why, I mean, you hardly know me."

Wayne smiled softly. "I do feel like I know you."

"It's odd," she said, "but I feel the same way. Like I've known you much longer than since I saw your truck and asked you for a ride. It's… so easy to talk to you even about hard things."

Wayne shrugged. "I guess you are the first person ever to feel that way. People usually don't share much with me because they…know me as this relaxed happy-go-lucky guy who doesn't take life too seriously."

Erin tilted her head. "Then they have the wrong impression of you. You are a very good listener. I can't thank you enough for all you've done for me already."

Wayne felt a warmth spread in his chest that was totally new to him. A connection with her that took his breath away. He stared at her beautiful face and he just wanted to keep looking. She had just said such nice things about him. As if she truly appreciated him.

Erin looked away. "We had better get back into town. I need to start making a plan for the flower arrangements and you could maybe call that lawyer and… I don't want to wait too long having no idea what my position is."

She shook her head. "I don't understand how he can simply have partied here with his family and friends, after he knew that… I had run because I found out about his cheating. Doesn't he have any sense of shame or…" She swallowed hard. "I guess it also proves he never cared one bit for me. He wasn't sorry at all that I ran. I mean… He was betraying me with Jenn, but he could still have cared for me somehow. That he…was just attracted to her physically. Without feeling a true bond like we had…" Tears formed in her eyes and she shook her head again, impatiently. "I don't want to cry about him. He was not worth it."

"But your dreams were," Wayne said softly. "You built an expectation of what your future would be like with him. It was a beautiful dream and you wanted to protect it. It was precious to you. Now it's all broken and… That is the pain you are feeling. That you ought to be feeling. What kind of person would not hurt for a lost dream? It means you are alive and…"

"I guess I should have known better. I had enough indications he wasn't trustworthy. It is good and nice to have dreams and want a future, but you have to be realistic." Erin wiped at her eyes. "I allowed myself to run after some fantasy, as if suddenly someone will love you, for you, accepting all your weaknesses and mistakes… Like it was meant to be and all. Now I know that is nonsense. People want to believe in it and it's promoted everywhere in movies and books, but it is not true. Not true."

She repeated the words with fervor, almost as if to convince herself.

Wayne reached out and took her hand in his. "Listen, Erin. Don't beat yourself up about having had dreams and expectations. That is normal. You shouldn't give up on them either."

"Well, I am. I am deciding here and now in this office at this desk where a manager told me that my ex celebrated our wedding without me that I am not believing in love anymore. That I don't want to believe in it. Because it only makes you vulnerable. It only hurts when it goes wrong. It is better not to expect anything of others and just trust in yourself and forge your own path in life."

Wayne squeezed her hand. "Maybe you are overreacting now."

"No." Erin pulled her hand free and rose from the chair. "It's just accepting reality. Throwing away the rose-colored glasses. Livia was right in that respect. You have to come to your senses, wake up. I have to accept that I couldn't make my dreams work. My dreams of living independently away from my family, having my own career and finding the love of my life. Maybe… I was running away again. Running away from what they wanted of me because I was afraid I could not live up to it.

But it's time to rethink things. To consider whether they were right after all and I belong with them in the family business. I don't want to be running for running's sake, you know." She forced a smile even though there were still tears on her lashes. "I guess Hutch's betrayal really shook up everything. Do I really want to be a wife? Do I really want to work in a flower shop and go home to cook dinner for my husband? Should I aspire to something more than that? A career in real estate, money, travel... There are so many places in the world that I haven't seen yet. So many experiences I haven't tried yet. I was born a Lakewood and my parents have always told me that I should be grateful for that. That I was privileged and that I should think of ways to make the most of everything I do in life. I don't know if I have been doing that. But I can think about it. Use this time, this time-out maybe, however you want to call it, to see what I can do."

Wayne wasn't sure he followed her reasoning. "You don't seem to get along very well with your sister. You indicated that she interferes in your life and choices. Why would you want to be a part of the family firm again, when they won't allow you to be yourself?"

"I don't know..." Erin's voice was shaky. "I

don't know if I have been myself the past few years. If the person doing the cruises and seeing the world and meeting Hutch and getting engaged, if that was truly me. Or if I was just playacting because I wanted to be like other people. Have the handsome guy, settle down… I don't know anything for certain anymore."

The pain in her voice hurt him too. "You mustn't uproot everything because of this one man."

"It was the man I was going to spend the rest of my life with. I intended to say *I do* and stick with him. I don't believe in breaking your marriage vows when trouble comes along. When I go in, I go all in."

He stared at the passion in her features and for a moment he wished that he had known such love. Someone choosing him for himself and saying: I am here to stay, I am not walking away when I am disappointed in you or I don't understand what you are doing. I am here for you. Because I care for you.

Erin said, "I never thought that I would marry Hutch and see if we could make it work. No. In my mind we were going to make it work, regardless, because we would have promised forever to each other. But now I see how naive that was. Because you need two people to make it work and Hutch was never committed to it. I don't know when he decided that, whether it was already decided when he first kissed me in the snow… It could just be the way he is. And I didn't see it. I didn't want to see it. I clung to my fantasy and…ultimately I was the one who let me down. I didn't prevent this from happening."

"You can't prevent everything. You…"

"Never mind, Wayne." She gave him a sad smile. "I have learned my lesson now. I should be far more careful and second-guess people's motives. I should even second-guess my own motives when I rush into something. I don't want to make the same mistakes over and over. I am too old for that and should be a little wiser too." She clenched her jaw and nodded as if to reaffirm a promise to herself. "I will try and do better. From now on."

CHAPTER TEN

APRIL LOOKED AT Erin as she sat at the kitchen table putting slices of carrot onto a buttered oven tray. It was supposed to become a vegetable dish for dinner but Erin's focus seemed to be somewhere else. She started on a row and then her hands fell silent and she stared at the tray with glazed eyes.

"Are you tired?" April asked softly. "You have been out and about all day long."

"Yes, I have been taking down notes for the flower arrangements in the community center. I've also talked to the farmers who will deliver the flowers. To make sure I know what material I will have to work with and what everyone's expectations are." She glanced up with a nervous look. "Maybe they are expecting too much of me. I'm not really that good."

"That's nonsense. I've seen your creations onboard and they were always fantastic. I'm sure the town will be very pleased with what you come up with."

"I hope so. I don't want to mess up the celebrations."

"I'm sure that the celebrations will be a huge success. People are really looking forward to them. In communities like these such events are a big deal."

"No pressure, huh?" Erin said.

April came to sit opposite her, grating the cheese to cover the vegetables with. She wanted to say something like *I can imagine how you must be feeling*, but to be honest she had no idea how it felt to be betrayed on your wedding day. It had to be terrible.

Erin said, "Are you close with Gina?"

April had to blink a moment to realize what she meant. Gina, her elder sister, of course. But why would Erin suddenly ask a question about their bond? It seemed totally off topic. Still she felt she had to give more than a casual reply.

"We used to be firm friends when we were younger and still living at home. We played with dolls together and we loved horses. We played in the orchards of course, hide-and-seek, and we had a tree house." April smiled at the happy memories. "Our relationship was uncomplicated. When we didn't like something, we simply said it and if we really had a fight, we would pinch or kick each other. That was straightforward enough. Of course Mom or Dad would tell us that we had to say we were sorry and had to make up, but the whole process of giving vent to hurt or anger seemed simple. Now it's more complicated." She frowned. "Gina was more of a pleaser while I liked to do my own things. So it was sometimes said to me that I had to be good like my sister. I didn't want to be like Gina or be loved for acting like Gina. I wanted to be loved for being me, you know." She shrugged with a little embarrassment. "Maybe it was different for you?"

"Livia is the ultimate big sister. Protective, always doing everything right." Erin looked serious. "It created a lot of tension when we still both worked in the family firm. Even though we were responsible for different tasks, it felt like we were always in each other's way. There was competition. I can't call it anything else."

April nodded. "I never felt much competition with Gina, but I did with Cade. My big brother who always knew better and who made all the decisions and who, when Dad died, took over the ranch and never asked whether I wanted to have a share or be involved or... It was all decided and I just had to accept it. I do love Cade very much but we have always had this… struggle to understand each other. To not get lost in the feelings on both sides. Cade thinks he has to protect me and care for me and make decisions for me and I want to be free and take care of my own life. We both mean well and when push comes to shove, we will always be there for each other, but…it can be tough to navigate the waters without too much turmoil."

Erin seemed relieved. "When I met your family and saw you together, it felt sort of… ideal."

April laughed. "Because you caught us at a good time. You know, Cade is married to Lily now and it's really made him softer and more open. Easier to talk to. And when I came back to Heartmont to live here, with my husband… I think it smoothed over a lot of old hurt. It made us a family again, who really trust each other. It feels good."

Erin nodded with a sad expression. "I wish I had that. A family that looks out for me. Not that my parents don't love and care… They do. They are wonderful people and I love them a lot, but…they are very socially conscious and from a young age we were told to watch what we did and what we said and what people might think of us. We had to perform to certain standards. I often felt quite restricted. That is one of the reasons I left to go cruising."

April nodded. "I can relate to that. Cruising was really a way out for me. To get away from Heartmont and everything that was holding me back. It helped me to discover more about myself and what I wanted, what made me happy..."

MATT STOOD AT the door leading into his kitchen area. He had been about to step through and kiss his wife, who was making dinner with their guest, when he had heard them talking about cruising. He had stopped in his tracks to hear a little more. He just knew that when he came in, they'd stop talking, change the subject or whatever, and he wanted to hear this.

He didn't want to eavesdrop or anything, just catch a little of the conversation. He knew why April had loved cruising. How hard she had worked to gain a coveted promotion. And then right at the time when she had been able to make that step, he had come back in her life and they had fallen in love and he had asked her to marry him. She had sacrificed a lot to be with him, to live here in a small town, run a hotel with him. Sometimes he wondered if she ever looked back and wished she was still working on the ship and seeing the world. "There is so much freedom in cruising," April said. "You are always waking up in a new place and able to see exciting things. The guests also have intriguing stories to share. It just breathes so much adventure."

Yes, adventure. April had always loved that. Even as a young woman when she had come to work for him after he had lost his wife in a plane accident and had been left to care for his young daughter alone, she had loved to do unexpected things, think up games for Belle, take them on picnics. She was creative and outgoing, someone who loved to be with other people. He didn't know if the simple life they led now, here on the ranch, sometimes restricted her. There was a longing in her voice as she spoke of cruising. It hurt him because it was a longing that was not directed at him. Because she might have wishes he could not fulfill.

"I'll just put the cheese on top," April said now, "and then it can go into the oven. Matt must be here soon."

Hearing his own name jolted him from his thoughts and with a guilty feeling he entered the room. "Hello, ladies."

April turned to him at once and smiled her

megawatt smile. It lit up her entire face. She wore an apron because she was cooking and he just loved that it was a little crooked and that there was a little grated cheese on her nose. If they had been alone, he would have rubbed it away with his finger and then kissed her. But Erin was here.

Erin had just suffered heartache and it wouldn't do to show off their wedded bliss in front of her.

At least…he experienced wedded bliss every single day. Was it the same for April? Or did she miss something, something he couldn't give her?

He helped to open the oven door so April could slide the tray in and she beamed up at him, giving him a little wink. She was probably as aware as he was that they couldn't act too loving in front of their guest, but still… He turned to Erin and said, "How was your day?"

"Long," she said with a sigh. "I was glad for the distraction and not having to just sit here all day and think about what went wrong, but… I am also tired now and a bit…. lost maybe. I met my sister Livia in town."

"Oh," April said, "that is why you asked me about Gina and me. I wondered." She cast Erin a look as if she wanted to know more about the meeting with Erin's sister but didn't know if she could ask.

Erin said, "Livia had found out I was getting married and she was upset about it. About me not inviting Mom and Dad and her to the wedding. It was very...challenging to see her. I mean, what could I say? I guess she does understand why I had decided not to ask them to come after all their criticism...but still..." She stared ahead, her jaw working.

Matt glanced at April. She was such a kind person who always felt for others having a hard time. He could see in her face how much she sympathized with Erin and wished she could make it all easier on her.

Erin said, "I had told myself over and over it was better not to ask them and that they would not even have wanted to come to a wedding they didn't agree with, but when I saw Livia, I realized that... I had really truly cut them out of my life, out of my future as I envisioned it. I had actually thought that I had no choice except to exclude them. It was hard. The odd thing is that as soon as she heard I had not married Hutch, she was hugging me and telling me that I could come back home and my parents would be so happy. I felt like she was immediately sucking me back into their world. Like a vortex that tried to pull me under. But I want to swim by myself for a bit, you know. Not follow someone else's plotted course for my life."

"That's understandable," Matt said. "And you have the chance to do so right here. You can stay with us for a while, work on the anniversary celebrations... Treat it like a time away from everything, just for you. You will feel better afterward. Whatever you may decide." He hesitated a moment and added, "I do think it's generous of your sister to invite you back. She could also have said that you had really hurt their feelings and the fact that the wedding didn't go through changed nothing about that."

"I know." Erin nodded at him. "I am super aware of that. How generous they are, and at the same time it doesn't feel like generosity, but more like...taking advantage of the situation to draw me back into a world that I was trying to escape. They never took my profile down from the company website. To their friends they pretended I was traveling the world, not mentioning I actually worked on a cruise ship. It felt like they never accepted what I chose, what I wanted to do. Now everything is set up for me to come back, just slip in the back door unnoticed and it will all be alright again. But it doesn't feel alright. I can't explain it but it sort of…makes me shy away. I don't want this, right now."

"Nobody says you have to decide about it, right now," April said in a reassuring voice. "I am sure your sister didn't mean to put pressure on you. Just to let you know the door is open on their part. That is a good thing, right? You don't need to apologize; they just love you."

Erin seemed to want to argue but then she slumped and just sat there with her head down. April went to the fridge. "I'll pour you something to drink. Sparkling water, lemonade?"

"Water is fine," Erin said in a dull voice.

April gave her a worried look. She poured the water and put it beside her, then gestured for Matt to follow her out of the kitchen. Once they were out of earshot, she whispered, "Why did you immediately have to say it is so generous and all? That family just wants Erin back with them, in the firm, but she was never happy there. Cruising gave her a chance to get away. She won't just go back to them now."

Her fervor took him by surprise. "Sorry. I just wanted her to feel better. Her fiancé might have betrayed her but her family are still there for her."

"I just don't know if they are being selfless

or they have a plan. It's never a good idea to be drawn into someone's plan for you. You have to make your own decisions. I feel like Erin never had a chance to do that. She should regroup now. See what she wants. Not the others."

"I understand. I'll stop offering free advice. I'm apparently just not that good at it."

April looked him in the eye, still all afire to say more, then suddenly her eyes filled with tenderness and she leaned into him and kissed him. "You are good at so many other things," she whispered.

Matt was happy as he kissed her back and counted himself a lucky man to have her. But there was a tiny bit of doubt left in the back of his mind. Was April's zeal to help her friend fight for her freedom dictated by her own adventurous nature and need to be free? He felt like he had found a wild horse in the mountains and had taken it home to keep it and care for it. That he loved it and was doing all he could to keep it happy with him but the horse still ached to run free.

He touched her face a moment, let his fingertips slide from her temple to her chin. She looked up at him, her eyes searching his expression. "What?" she asked softly.

She always knew right away when something was on his mind.

He shrugged it off and smiled. “Nothing. I love you.”

“I love you too.”

CHAPTER ELEVEN

ERIN AWOKE EARLY the next day and as soon as the sweetness of sleep subsided, that nice lazy drowsy feeling that everything was alright with the world, reality intruded, shocking her upright in bed. What had happened to her? Had Hutch really kissed Jenn? Or had it just been a bad dream? It had to be. All she had done afterward, run away, meet Wayne, flee to Heartmont, it seemed like something out of someone else's story. She normally never took instant decisions or trusted strangers with her hurt. But now she had been forced to do it.

Erin sat with her eyes closed, trying to breathe deeply. She couldn't bear to think of herself waking up like this, again and again, from now on. Constantly being confronted with her own failure, her sense of inadequacy. Panic clawed its way through her chest. She could simply not solve this situation in any way which would make her feel better. It was just one big mess and wherever Hutch was, he was laughing at her. He had partied with all of his pals at her expense!

Now anger mixed with the pain and drove her to open her eyes and reach for her phone. There was one thing she could do. Get even with him for the hurt he had caused her by sending the bill to her parents. He had pretended to the manager it was just a measure to ensure the costs would be covered, but she knew he had really done it to alert her parents to her decision to exclude them. He'd destroyed his relationship with Erin so he'd decided to destroy the one she had with her parents. Admittedly, it had been under strain already, but this blow would really have ruined things. He hadn't wanted her to have anything left.

But she would get even with him for that. She would send the bill to his firm. The one he had started with that college friend, which he had been so proud of. She would make sure that the money he earned went to paying for their big day. Because he had also been a part of it and he needed to pay his dues.

She didn't know exactly what the address of their company was. He had shown her the building where the office was from the outside, pointing up to the third floor. He had told her that the space was still being refurbished and the painters and decorators didn't want them traipsing around and ruining things so they had simply stood there on the pavement together gazing up. She had felt so happy, so looking forward to being settled.

It hurt to remember that now. To think back on the naive woman she had been to trust him. It almost seemed like part of the problem was her willingness to just believe everything he told her about how much he loved her.

Erin forced herself to look for the address online. There it was, the building. And then she needed to see if she could find the exact address of Hutch's business. Oh, the building had its own website where all the businesses housed inside it were listed. She would just have to look up the name of Hutch's firm. Watts and Michaels. Hutch had been upset his name would be second but it was commonplace to put the longer name last because it sounded better. But he had told her that it would be mainly him doing all the work because his buddy was inexperienced. As if he had had the experience… Anyway…

She looked under the *W* but didn't find Watts and Michaels. Had he changed the names after all? Nope, nothing under the *M* either. That was odd. Was she missing something?

After going over the site again she decided to simply call the reception desk. The number was on the homepage. While she waited for someone to pick up the phone, she willed herself to use a professional voice and sound detached, not like some worked-up ex after money.

A friendly voice asked how they might help her.

"I would like to know the exact address, I mean, the suite number assigned to Watts & Michaels. It could also be Michaels & Watts. I'm not sure of the order."

"I will have a look. Do you happen to know the floor they are on?"

"Third floor."

She had stared at that window, so happy her soon-to-be husband had found a new profession so quickly. Even as the rain had started to fall she had felt warm and safe leaning against Hutch. She had so not seen this coming.

"Miss? I am sorry but I can't find any such firm. Are you sure you have the right building? There are a lot of office buildings on this block."

"Uhm..." Erin's heart suddenly beat very fast. Had she made a mistake? Or was the truth something else altogether?

"I could be mistaken," she said quickly. "I will make more calls. Thank you. Sorry to have bothered you."

"Not at all. Good luck finding them. Have a nice day."

Yes, good luck finding them… Erin searched online for Watts and Michaels, tried the business bureau, even social media. No trace of them. As if they didn't exist.

As if? Make that: *because* they didn't exist. Hutch hadn't just lied to her about loving her. He had also lied to her about having a business.

She sat on the bed in shock. Really? He had invented a business? He had invented work, a day job he could pretend to go to in the mornings while in reality he…

Yes, what would he have done?

Had he just made it up to give her the impression he would also bring in money? Had it been a matter of his ego getting hurt if he was unemployed while she worked? That was sort of understandable.

In any case, a better reason than assuming that he had never intended to work at all. That he had figured she might as well pay the bills.

She could just see how it would have gone. "Hi honey, how was your day?"

"Not so good. We are having so much difficulty getting started. Clients are hard to find." Or: "Someone pulled out at the last instant and now we've lost money."

Whatever the reason, he would have told her that there was no way he could pay bills this month. But she had her salary, right? And maybe some savings? He'd make it up to her later, of course. Once the business was doing better.

She closed her eyes again. How long would he have strung her along like that? Making her pay for everything while he just freewheeled and had a good time with his friends. Or with girlfriends too, maybe. What did she know?

His firm didn't exist. He had lied about everything. He had built this entire future with her like a house of cards. Once you pulled at one card, the entire thing came crashing down.

It made her feel even worse about her own gullibility. But…it also meant she could not bill his business for the wedding party expenses. Because there was no business. She was grasping at straws. And she could hear Hutch laughing in the distance.

Her phone rang. The sound startled her so much she let it drop. Fortunately it landed on the duvet. The screen lit with a soft glow and the name Wayne.

Wayne.

Wayne? Did she even want to talk to him now? She felt like packing up her things and running away from here, hiding from everyone who knew her until she stopped feeling so bad.

The phone kept ringing and she swiped the call away.

A moment later a text message appeared on the screen. Want to have breakfast at my place? My dog has puppies. They are the absolute cutest. Come on over and have a look. W

Puppies sounded great. Breakfast was nice too. She just didn't know what to say to him when he asked her how she was. If she said worse it might sound very melodramatic. Still, that was exactly how she felt.

Another message came in. I can come and pick you up. I keep forgetting you have no car there.

She replied at once, Don't worry, April offered me her car whenever I need it. She is here most of the time anyway caring for the guests. I will be there in say…twenty minutes? I look forward to seeing the dogs. E

WAYNE LOOKED AT the screen of his phone. He rarely felt this excited when he received a message from someone. Usually it just meant work.

A neighbor with a leaky roof, a chore having to do with his work on the committee. The anniversary celebrations had delivered loads of work ever since the start of the year. But this was one message he was eager to see. His eyes raced over the text. She was coming! She looked forward to seeing the puppies.

The puppies, pal, not you. He put the phone away and looked around his kitchen. It had a nice country feel to it with woodwork around the built-in appliances but it was very sparse decoration-wise. He didn't have a calendar on the wall with daily wisdom, no figurines anywhere, or vases of flowers. It was all very empty and practical, not very…inviting to a female visitor. Then there was also the small matter of last night's dinner dishes left in the sink…

Wayne got to his feet and hurried to clean those dishes, make the sink shine and set the table at the center of the kitchen for a breakfast for two. While he was at it, he realized how odd this was. He never invited women to his home. When he dated, which he had done less and less over the past few years, he always met the women in town, where they could have dinner or watch a movie. He had gone on active dates, rock climbing and horse riding. Even wild water rafting. But he had never ever invited a woman into the privacy of his home. This was his place, his man cave, his castle. Nobody came here, except for other men from the community when they had to ask something or borrow something. When they came to offer him cattle or discuss a difficult horse. Or…he smiled at the box in the corner. When they were interested in one of his puppies.

He bred cattle dogs on a very small scale. He had two mother dogs whom he loved to bits and who were excellent cattle workers. Every now and then he contacted someone via the cattle dog club who had a male that would make a nice combination. He cared for the puppies, making sure they were socialized and housebroken before he sold them. Anyone who wanted one of his pups had to prove they knew what a cattle dog was all about. That they were working dogs and needed a purpose in life. Otherwise the dog would just sit around at home and eat the couch.

He sat down beside the box that functioned as shelter for the litter and scratched Birch behind her ears. She was the eldest of his two dogs, the mother of the other one. Birch had been but a puppy herself when he had bought her and brought her home to keep him company and help him on the ranch. She had been a perky little thing from the start, not afraid of cows and other animals much bigger than she was. She was very curious and a great learner. Even now that he had worked with her for many years he still taught her new hand signals every week. It kept her on her toes and she loved that. But when she was nursing her puppies he treated her differently, gave her the princess treatment. And she loved that as well.

He grinned as he pushed back her left ear. "Good morning, little mommy. How are we today? Everything alright with the little ones? I am surprised every time how tiny they actually are when they are born and how quickly they get older, bigger, bolder. Just look at them now." He used his other hand to carefully touch the pups that were scrambling over each other. Birch was a very gentle dog and she knew he meant well, but even she could be protective when her young were at stake. He always took care to approach them with caution and not just try and grab one.

"Hello little one..." It was that same pup again, the one with a brownish ring around his left eye, that caught his attention. It was like the doggy focused on him as soon as he was near. The others were busy playing with each other or just taking a nap, but this one seemed to really want to interact right away. He was curious and incredibly playful. This one was special.

Birch perked up and turned her head toward the back door. Wayne now also heard the sound of an engine coming into the yard. She had detected it before he did. That Erin was coming.

"Erin is someone you will like, Birch," he said softly. "She is tough because she has to be, but she also has a softer side. She is a bit sad now so you will have to cheer her up. You and the pups."

Birch gave him a knowing look. A bit conspiratorial in fact. He grinned as he rose to his feet. It would be great for them to help Erin without her even noticing.

ERIN PARKED AND got out of April's car. When she had decided to take Wayne's invitation, she had felt a little better. Why sit at the ranch hotel feeling sorry for herself when she could go out and do something? This was a beautiful area and she had not seen much of it yet.

Now as she stood in the morning sunshine looking around her, she almost felt like she had traveled back in time. This was a traditional ranch house with barns and stables, she could hear horses neighing in the distance. A young man just went into one of the barns, wearing overalls. He had to be Wayne's ranch hand. He had mentioned that he had hired one since he was doing so much work for the anniversary celebrations. It was nice that he could afford to hire someone so he could invest his own time in the community. It proved that he had a good heart.

He may have a good heart but he did have a very…austere home. She didn't see any curtains in front of the windows, not a nice bench on the porch where he could sit at night to enjoy the evening air and look at the moon. There was a broom there and other useful equipment but nothing suggesting he could unwind here.

Then again, with his cattle, horses and dogs, he probably had little time to relax. He had to be forever working.

It was strange to think that his father had considered this kind of life not worth much. To her it seemed like a very calming experience. Start the day as the sun came up and work with the seasons…it had to feel very natural. It was a world away from the rush of the city and all that seemed so terribly important there. She had always loved the bustle, the constant activity around her and the feeling she could step out and be part of something new. On the cruise ship that had been the same. It was a world in itself, offering all kinds of entertainment. She had been fully immersed in that life in the fast lane, never attuning herself to a calmer rhythm. But standing here she wondered what it would be like.

"Hey, good morning!" Wayne appeared on the porch. He wore a dark blue shirt with stonewashed jeans. His feet were stuck in beige boots. He leaned against one of the porch supports and smiled at her. As the sunshine caressed his features and his dark hair and lit his eyes, it struck her what a good-looking guy he really was. The kind of handsome cowboy you'd expect on a ranch like this.

She blinked a moment to dispel the notion. Two days ago she had been about to marry Hutch. He was a completely different type of man. Wayne was definitely not someone she'd ever…

Look at? Consider partner material?

This is super awkward, she told herself. A flush crept into her cheeks. It had to be because she was so emotionally vulnerable that she felt an attraction she would normally not feel. It had to do with the way in which Wayne had appeared in her life, like the knight in shining armor to take her away from it all. He had offered help when she had needed it most. That was why she felt connected to him. It had nothing to do with a real feeling. It was just the result of all these stressful events.

Wayne gestured for her to come on over. "Welcome to the ranch," he said with a somewhat nervous smile. It felt like he cared a lot what she would think of his place. Now it was normal to want to show off what you yourself were proud of. But with him it seemed to be a little more. As if her opinion mattered a lot. Was it because she had worked in real estate and could judge the value of properties? Or…

She forced herself to walk quickly so she didn't have to complete the thought. Her empty stomach was causing some weird sensations. She needed to get inside and have that breakfast he had promised her.

Wayne said, "Was it easy to find?"

"Oh yes, April had given me very clear directions. I told her at first that I could use the car navigation but she laughed and said that the addresses here are often not known to the system."

"Exactly. I'm glad you found it easily. Come on inside. Then you can meet Birch."

"Birch?"

"My dog, the mother of the puppies. She is a very kind creature."

"Even when she has babies? I have heard dogs can get quite protective then."

"I will be right there beside you to comfort her. She'll immediately understand you are a friend."

Erin looked up into his eyes. "Is that what I am? A friend? We only met two days ago."

"I know, but it seems like it was much longer." He held her gaze. "To me it feels as if I have known you…for months. Like I…know I can trust you."

"Trust me?" Erin echoed. "How do you mean? I had to trust in you when I got into your truck after running from Hutch and the party. You never had to trust me."

"Yes I had to." He pointed at his door. "I don't receive a lot of visitors. People from town drop by when they need something but… It is rarely social. This breakfast is. I really look forward to it."

She didn't know what to say. It was like he was suddenly singling her out, making her feel very special. This was his home, his fortress, which he apparently kept very much to himself. He had to feel a closeness to somone to invite them over and open up And now she was here. Asked to come on inside and eat with him.

She stepped across the threshold with a sense

of anticipation. Inside things were mainly wood as well. The floor, the wall paneling, the ceilings. It gave a warm natural atmosphere. To the right was an archway leading into a sitting area with large leather couches and a fireplace. To the left a similar archway led into a kitchen space. Modern appliances were built into the wood to keep the ranch style alive. On the table in the heart of it stood bread, cold cuts, cheeses, jam, butter and a large pot of coffee. She could smell it in the air. Her stomach growled.

Wayne grinned. "We have to eat first, I think, and look at the dogs later."

"Nothing is going to keep me away from those puppies. Where are they?"

CHAPTER TWELVE

"COME ON OVER HERE," he said, and gestured for her to follow him to a box in the corner. The head of a border collie peered up at her, its amber eyes searching her expression. The puppies were playing beside her. "They are so cute!" she exclaimed, slowly lowering herself to a sitting position. "Especially that one." She made sure not to point directly at the doggy, but to motion in his direction.

Wayne smiled as he leaned down over her. "That one is something else. He is so curious and he listens to all the sounds and… I can just see he will be an amazing cattle dog. I hope I can find a home for him where he can really work. Not someone who takes him to agility training on a Saturday. These dogs need to work every single day of their lives. That is what makes them happy."

"What kind of work do they do exactly?"

"Herd sheep or cows. Join their masters during horse rides. Some are trained to search for water, for natural sources of water on the land. There is so much these dogs can do. They are very intelligent and have a huge learning capacity."

"So they are easy to train?" Erin asked.

Wayne laughed softly. "I never said that."

"But if they are so smart and can learn so much, why would it not be easy?"

"Because they also have a personality. They can be quite stubborn when they want to. Some can become obsessive and display herding behavior when you don't want them to. Where they go and chase cars or kids on bicycles. It's always a fine line between raising a great cattle dog and spoiling it completely by the wrong approach."

"It almost sounds like raising children," Erin said, watching the puppies.

"I think that is a good comparison. You want your children to learn something and do better when they make a mistake, but you have to think about the way in which you teach them things. Not by force or harshness. The no result no reward method. It can be very damaging."

"Was your dad like that?" she asked softly. She didn't look at him but kept staring at the dogs.

Wayne didn't reply at once. She listened to

his quiet breathing beside her. She thought he wanted to ignore her question, just let time pass until he could start talking about something else. But then he said, "My father was never unfair with us, I suppose. He didn't beat us or anything. I had a classmate who did get beaten at home when his dad didn't like his behavior so I guess I have always been grateful my father wasn't like that. But he wasn't very patient either. If he had told you to do something, you'd better have listened so you could do what he wanted without having to ask again what he had meant. He also used to say that a man keeps his promises. Which to his mind was like: if I ask you something and you've said yes, that is forever. Like, as a kid he asked me whether I would study hard and make him proud. Of course I said yes. What kid would not have? I wanted him to be proud of me, to love me."

The tremor in Wayne's voice touched Erin's heart. She knew what it was like to try and please your parents and to never really succeed at it too.

Wayne continued, "I made the promise and I meant it. But over time when I figured out that book learning was not my thing and going to college would just mean four years of agony for a degree I had no use for anyway, I made my own decisions. My dad was so disappointed. He reminded me of that promise of old and said I had to keep my word. I told him things had changed. *I haven't changed*, he said. *My expectations haven't changed. You changed. You let me down.*"

Erin now looked at Wayne. She caught the flash of hurt in his face. She reached out quickly and put her hand on his arm. "He was mistaken. You are a great person. You did what you had to do but it hurt no one. It wasn't your fault that he was disappointed."

"Wasn't it?" Wayne looked her in the eye. His jaw worked hard. "I could have done what he asked of me. I could have gone to college and got a degree and found a job he liked."

"And be unhappy for all of your life just because he wanted you to follow that path?"

"Maybe. He sacrificed a lot for us. He raised us singlehandedly. It was a hard life being a man on his own with a full-time business and two boys. He must have felt like it was too much at times. But he kept on going for our sakes. Alex made himself into the person Dad always wanted us to be. But me..."

"Your father must have raised you both to

become responsible men. To have a fulfilling life. To do things you loved, pursue dreams."

Wayne laughed softly. "This can't be a dream according to my father. This…ramshackle ranch as he calls it is a place you'd only take on when you had to, not a property you'd want to buy. He believed he could offer us much more and saved hard for both of our college tuitions. I did let him down. And he will never stop making me feel that way."

"Then you have to decide not to let it hurt you anymore." Erin said it with an earnest intensity keeping her hand on his arm. "You cannot spend your entire life working off guilt over your choices. You did what was right for you. It's too bad your father doesn't understand but… You don't owe him—"

"But I do," Wayne said in a harsh tone. "I do owe him. He did so much for Alex and me. I know that. And still I feel like…he could have been a different father and I would have had a different life." He rose to his feet abruptly, making Birch perk her head up to look at him. Erin could have sworn she saw concern in the dog's features. As if she sensed that her boss was hurting and she didn't want him to…

Wayne walked to the table where breakfast was laid out. "Shall we eat now? The coffee is getting cold. We also have work to do in town later."

Erin felt an odd disappointment that he didn't want to confide in her, seemed almost uncomfortable with the conversation, but he was a man and to her knowledge men didn't easily open up about feelings. Maybe it was very special as it was that he had told her something.

After all, they barely knew each other.

Still, he had said it was like they had known each other for months. Which was true, because she also felt that way. She had opened up to him about her feelings in a way she never had to other people. What was happening here?

She sat down and he poured her coffee and made fresh toast. "I hope April didn't mind that you left?" he asked. "She might have wanted you to breakfast there."

"She didn't say so. There was a group of hotel guests leaving and she was very busy. I think she was glad for me to get out and about for a bit. I uh…" Erin took a deep breath.

"Didn't sleep well?" he queried with a probing look.

"Oh, sleep was fine. Waking up was the problem. I remembered the whole mess and…" She put jam on her toast and spread it with her knife. "I thought I could get even with Hutch by billing the wedding party he and his friends indulged in to his business. I knew where it was, but not the exact address—it's in one of those large buildings where there are offices on every floor—so I tried to find more information online. Then I discovered that there is no business. He lied to me about that too." She forced a laugh. "Maybe his name isn't even Hutch Michaels, huh? Who knows? Great, Erin, you were engaged to a con man."

"That is not your fault."

"But it is. I fell for him. I wanted to believe him. People warned me about him and I pushed on anyway. I caused all of this." She sighed. "My grandma used to say when you burn yourself, you get blisters. And she's right. I burned myself and now I am dealing with blisters all around."

"But you don't have to do it alone," Wayne said. He got up to get his phone from the sideboard. "I'll call my lawyer friend right now to ask what he suggests." Before she could even protest he placed the call. She ate in silence waiting for the call to be answered. Wayne explained in a few words that he had a friend who was cheated on by her fiancé hours before the wedding and that she had walked away but the wedding party had gone on anyway without her and she had now been billed for the expenses. He listened intently to what his contact was saying. Then he nodded and said, "Will do. Talk to you soon." He disconnected. "He said he needs more details so he is sending me an email with a few questions and if I could pass it on to you..." He grinned at her. "I need your email address even though you are sitting right across the table."

She also had to laugh. "You need it anyway for the anniversary celebrations. In case you need to forward emails from others with information. You know."

He nodded, then added the address to his address book. He put the phone aside. "We really have to enjoy breakfast and not just talk business. That ex of yours took away enough joy from your life. We won't let him have any more."

With these words a calm filled Erin's mind. Wayne was so right. Hutch had ruined so much and by being so anxious about it all she was giving him even more of her time and energy. It had to stop right here and now. She didn't want to think about him or about Livia and the question of where her sister had gone when she had left her at the community center.

Looking back, she wished she hadn't been

so rude to her. Livia might have meant well. Maybe she should call her at some point? To tell her she was sorry for the way in which their meeting had panned out? That it had been the stress of the whole situation. But she did want to patch things up with her family. Regardless of where her future lay, in the Lakewood company or not, she did want to make things better with Livia and with Mom and Dad. She had to think about the best way to go about it.

But right now she wanted to focus on other things. On sitting here over a delicious big breakfast prepared by a friend.

Yes, despite their short acquaintance she felt like Wayne was a true friend. Because he had acted like one. He had her back when she needed him. And she hoped she could do something for him in return. Help him with the preparations for the anniversary celebrations. And help him maybe…start believing in his choices a bit more? In what he had built here which he should be very proud of? It was sad that his father had rejected his choices in life so harshly. It soured the happiness Wayne could have here and that was not right. She had to show him somehow.

There was a brief knock on the back door and the ranch hand she had seen before entered. He looked worried. He held up his right arm. The wrist and underarm looked reddened. "That filly of yours came for me when I walked past her box. I could just jump away but slammed my arm into the box door opposite. Now these are just bruises but if she had caught me with her teeth..." He shook his head. "I am sorry to say, Wayne, but you have overreached with this one. She is so nervous and afraid of people. You can't help her. She will just snap at you until you get hurt."

Erin sat up straighter, trying to fill in the blanks. Wayne was obviously caring for a horse that was afraid and violent as a result. Why had he taken the mare in? Was she his horse from the start or...

A hundred questions crowded her mind. But she waited until the ranch hand had received some instructions and left again before she said, "So besides dogs and cows, you also have horses?"

"Just two at the moment. A really sweet elderly mare whose owner had to let her go because it became too expensive to keep her but he didn't want to have her killed. She can live here for the rest of her days." He smiled with warmth in his eyes. "She deserves that. She has done so much in her long life: has been a show jumper, later kids learned how to ride on her back. She gave much to people and now we have to give back to her. Keep her even when she can't earn her keep anymore."

"What about the other one?" Erin asked, reaching for an apple from the fruit bowl.

Wayne's eyes darkened. "The other one," he said with a sigh. "That is a different story. She was found roaming someone's land. She was very afraid and they didn't know what to do with her. I was with a pal when the news was messaged and I heard they were thinking of shooting her."

"What?" Erin said.

Wayne lifted a hand to stop her from exploding in indignation. "Think about it. She's a horse that's very afraid and unreliable and she's roaming a rancher's land. She's causing terror with his cattle, coming near his house where his kids are. He is merely thinking about potential risks. The horse is not his so what can he do?"

"Try and catch it, calm it."

Wayne laughed softly. "That is what I suggested and they just said I was nuts. It would cost money and who would take care of her once she was caught?"

Erin held his gaze. "I know the answer to the latter question. She is here with you now."

"Yes. I went over and I spent two days with her to get her to trust me enough so I could approach her and lead her away off the man's land into a corral. Then I spent more time with her to get her to trust me enough so I could move her here. Now she is here and I try to make her see that not every movement near her is a danger to her."

"That sounds like this is going to be a long process."

Wayne shrugged. "All things in life take time. I mean, when it's worth something you are willing to put the time into. She's a beautiful horse." He gestured at her apple. "Once you're done eating, we can go and see her."

"Won't she get startled?"

"Probably. First few days she was here, I avoided every kind of interaction that could make her freak out. But then I realized that it wasn't teaching her anything. She has to start believing that regardless of what scares her she is safe with me. So she has all of these experiences from a storm outside or a person coming near her and...hopefully she will get less skittish over time."

"How much time will be needed?"

Wayne shrugged again. "You never know. I pay for her food and shelter and she can figure it out in her own time. I just have to ensure my ranch hand doesn't get hurt. That is my responsibility as well." His expression clouded over a moment. "In fact, her being unreliable around my hired help could mean she has to adjust quicker than I would want her to. Or I will just have to start doing everything on my own again." He seemed to consider then shrugged it off and rose with energy. "Come on, I want you to see her."

They went outside and over to the stable building. The ranch hand was just carting away a wagon full of manure. Another dog followed him like a shadow.

"That is Frey, my other dog. She is a daughter of Birch. Her name is spelled with a *y* at the end, but pronounced Free. I love to call my dog by that name." He smiled at Erin. "Dogs are really free creatures you know. They run and play, don't have a care in the world. That is how we should also live. Taking after their example."

"They don't have to pay taxes," Erin said. She wanted the topic to stay light but still she added after a moment's hesitance, "They don't have complicated relationships. They don't fall in love with someone who leaves them at the altar."

"Technically you left him at the altar."

"I mean that their lives are so much simpler than ours. They have every reason to just frolic and be happy."

"But you can be happy too, Erin." Wayne held her gaze with an urgent look. "I want you to be happy."

She stared into his eyes, seeing in those depths how much he meant this. He really wanted the best for her, and it hurt him that she wasn't happy even though she should be. It touched her inside that he cared so much for her. Why anyway as he barely knew her?

She cleared her throat and said, "Where is that horse of yours?"

WAYNE BLINKED AND forced himself to look away, to lead her inside the stable building and show her around. But his thoughts weren't really focused. He liked having her here way too much. To sit and eat together, chat together, discuss something light or serious. It was easy with her. She was interested in his way of life.

Yes, because it is a novelty to her, he reminded himself. *She is a city girl who has landed in a small-town community almost by mistake. Just because she needed a place to hide from her hurting for a bit. To do something meaningful and find her feet again. She never chose to be here. It is just a detour from her real life. You have to keep that in mind. You can be nice to her, help her along, but the intention is to help her leave again. For a life that is cut out for her. Or that she is cut out for. Whatever.*

It gave him a sense of loss to think of her leaving. And he didn't need think about that right now. She was here for the moment, to see his horses and to discuss what they were going to do with the floral arrangements. He could enjoy her company and see what happened next. After all, he had never been much of a planner. Not one to take life too seriously. He believed that things turned out well in the end if you just kept trying for what you believed in. It would be okay for Erin too. She just needed to regroup.

Maybe also make up with her parents. He sensed that she was sad about the distance between them. And he had also sensed genuine concern in her sister Livia. There had to be some way to get them back together again. Not all family relationships were like Wayne's with his father: broken beyond repair. Stranded in too many high expectations and failed conversations. Too many assumptions about the other. Just because he knew how easy it was to end up stuck, he wanted to help her move things along. That was good for both her and her family.

And what about you? a small voice inside asked. *If you help her patch things up, she will leave town. She will go back into the family firm or even if she doesn't, she won't stick around here. Whatever bond you are building with her, it won't last.*

It hurt to think about her leaving. Hurt more than he wanted to acknowledge. But what choice did he have? Not helping her wasn't an option. He cared too much to just let her stew. He wanted her to be happy. Even if it meant that she was walking away from him.

CHAPTER THIRTEEN

INSIDE THE STABLE building the light was dimmer and Erin's eyes needed a few moments to adjust. She breathed the scent of hay and horses and a welcome calm settled in her center. This was such a beautiful place where she felt really connected with nature and the greater world around the ranch. With everything from the blue sky to the snowcapped mountains in the distance. Yes, even those mountains that had been part of her misadventure with Hutch were now a comforting presence, watching over them as they spent time here together. She wanted to spend more time with Wayne. Somehow his company healed something inside of her. The rawness of the betrayal was not so bad when he was with her, talking to her and lifting her up.

That was the main thing, she guessed. Hutch had never lifted her up. He had even sometimes torn her down with criticism or by not standing up for her when others were unkind. But Wayne was totally different. He always had a friendly word for her or supported her by just being by her side.

"There she is," Wayne said as he pointed ahead to a box. "I can already hear that she is stressed. It's her breathing."

Erin nodded although she didn't hear anything special. She wasn't attuned to a horse's body language as Wayne apparently was. She looked at him as he approached the box carefully. The focus in his eyes, the sadness that flashed across his features as he watched the animal he longed to help but who wasn't ready to accept that help.

With a shock she realized something. Maybe in a strange way their meeting hadn't just been for her sake, but for his. Maybe he also needed help, not because he was on the run from a wedding, but because he was all alone in what he did. Maybe he could also use a helping hand, a supportive word, a sense that he had someone to turn to.

"She is very pretty," she said softly, watching the dark brown horse with the small head and long mane.

"She should be out there in the fields, running." Wayne sounded dejected. "But I don't really trust her mood at the moment. I'm worried that she will try to break free and run away. Because she is so traumatized after what she's been through. I keep her in here for her own protection, until she starts to mellow. But when I see her like this, I feel like… I'm keeping her captive and I am not helping her at all." He reached up and rubbed his face. "I'm not a professional at this. I'm no trained horse therapist. Sure, over time I gained experience and I know a lot more than when I started out working with animals but…when I have a case like this, it feels like I am back at square one. Out of my depths and not knowing what to do."

"Love goes a long way," Erin said softly.

"Yes, but sometimes it just might not be enough. You can have all the knowledge from past experiences and still something doesn't quite click, come together. Or… I don't know." Wayne shook his head. "Maybe I lack patience. These things take time. I just feel sorry for her to see her in this state and I want to change everything overnight."

"I feel sorry too. But you're doing all you can. I'm sure she knows that." Erin touched Wayne's arm. "You are a really warmhearted, kind guy."

Wayne looked her in the eye. The subdued

light in the stable played across his features, made all the lines in his face softer. He half smiled and her heart did a little leap at the idea she could cheer him up and make this easier on him. He deserved to feel happier about his life than he did right now.

WAYNE STARED AT ERIN. When she smiled at him like that, something in his brain refused to continue thinking logically. He just wanted to stand here and look at her and feel so connected. In place, at ease. It was strange but it was like he had known her much longer than a few days. As if she somehow fitted in his life.

But that wasn't true, of course. She was here to help out, she was going to leave again. She was a city girl who might marvel at a rancher's lifestyle, enjoying it for a while since it was completely different from what she knew. But she had no roots here, and a single accepted invitation to breakfast didn't mean that she was interested in putting down any. She hurt after having lost her fiancé, her dreams of marriage, a life with this man and... He had to keep reminding himself of those facts. Or he might do something irresponsible.

Wayne turned away abruptly. "We should get into town to continue with our work for the anniversary," he said. "Have you been able to get some ideas for the displays?"

Erin seemed taken aback by his change of subject. She was silent for a moment and part of him hoped that she would say that she didn't want to work today but that they could take a walk or go horse riding or do something fun together. But instead she started talking about some sketches she had made.

He only listened half-heartedly, and said nothing but *hm* and *oh really?*

Outside the stable building as they walked back to the house, she stopped a moment to look at the rosebush that grew against the side of the house. "Those are very beautiful roses. What an unusual color. It's not quite pink or apricot or... I have never seen anything like it."

"It's a bush my grandparents grew at their place. My maternal grandparents. We weren't much in touch with them after my mother died, but we did go there once or twice a year usually for Christmas and the summer vacation. In summer the bush was always in full bloom. I loved it because my mother had loved it and when I started this place here, I asked my grandmother for a shoot to grow my own."

Erin smiled gently at the flowers. "It's very special. I love it."

"You know what?" Wayne said. "If you have a place in your display, you can use a few of these roses."

"Are you sure?"

"Yes. I want to give them to the community." He wanted her to work with them, to touch them with tender fingers and work them into her display. He wanted something of his to be mixed with something of hers and…

Maybe he was getting carried away by emotions? He was normally not this sentimental.

Erin said, "That is very sweet of you, Wayne. I'd love to think of something special to do with them. If you are sure you can spare me a few."

"You see how full the bush is. I have more than enough. You do with them what you want. You are the flower specialist."

Wayne gave his ranch hand instructions before they got into the truck to leave for town.

As they turned into the main road leading to Heartmont, Erin touched the silver horse charm that dangled from his rearview mirror. "Your mother also loved horses or she would not have worn this on a necklace. If she could have seen your ranch and what you do for horses, she would have been so proud of you."

Wayne's eyes grew moist. He blinked to stay

focused on the road. He wanted to say something, but his voice failed him. Erin was silent too. She didn't add anything to her compliment to cover the awkward silence. In fact, with her the silence wasn't awkward at all. He was glad she sat beside him and they shared these moments. He didn't feel like he had to pretend with her.

It was overwhelming to feel so at ease with someone. To realize that maybe…opening up could be easier than he had ever imagined.

But at the same time fear breathed through his heart. What was he doing opening up to someone who would vanish from his life again? Someone who wasn't even here by choice? She had landed here because of events outside of her control. She was caught up in so much turmoil. The situation with her ex, with her parents and her sister… She could probably not think straight. He had to ensure that he didn't make it harder for her by showing her any of his feelings. By adding to the complications because…he was falling for her?

No. He was definitely not falling for her. She was pretty and spontaneous and funny and warm. She was everything he wanted in a woman. But she wasn't the right one for him. He had always known that it asked a lot of a woman to marry a rancher who worked long hours and who couldn't just pick up and leave for a romantic holiday. Ranchers were also usually tough guys who didn't talk about feelings much and women wanted another type of man. Straight out of a movie.

In fact, when he had dated he'd often heard from women that it just wouldn't work between them, but he had never been able to figure out what they wanted of him. But whatever it was, he wasn't able to give it. Others could. Even his buddy Cade, not exactly the most sensitive or communicative man in the district, had found love. Wayne was happy for him and Lily, but he had wondered how on earth Cade had convinced Lily to fall in love with him.

When he saw happy couples like Cade and Lily, or Gina and that ranger of hers, it just seemed to be so natural between them, an understanding without words. They only had to look at each other to know what the other one wanted. He felt like he had never had such easy relationships. There had always been too many expectations he couldn't meet. The sense of dejection that came with that, the sense of failure, had once been overwhelming. He had let down his father, his brother, maybe even his mother because he hadn't done what Dad wanted, with school, going to college. Nobody had cared what was right for him as long as he did what they wanted.

Today it was all in the past and he could tell himself it didn't matter anymore. But it had changed him…

"I hope you don't think I am intruding," Erin said softly. She cast him a worried look. "You shared something very personal with me and maybe I am overstepping a boundary by referring to it, but… I felt you should know what I think." Her expression was honest, open, vulnerable.

Wayne swallowed hard. "You are not intruding. I mean… I shared with you because I trust you. You are different from anyone I ever met."

Erin flushed. "I am not that special."

"But you are. You just don't see it yourself."

"If I am that special, then why did Hutch betray me with other women? I know there must have been more than just Jenn. I denied it to myself but… I realize now he was never faithful."

"I have no idea why men are like that," Wayne said, clenching the wheel at the thought of her hurt for that guy who wasn't worth it. "But something inside of them causes it. The need to conquer maybe or to be admired. It doesn't reflect on you. I am sure of that."

Erin smiled weakly. "Thanks for the vote of confidence."

"I mean it. It is *his* issue, his problem. Some people are just…" Wayne looked for the right words to make his point without burning Hutch to the ground. He disliked the guy enough to blacken him top to bottom, but he realized that Erin needed a more nuanced approach to accept his reasoning. "Some people lie. Not to hurt others even, but just to make things better for themselves. They make their grades a little better or they have always caught the biggest fish… Once they realize that people are drawn to them because of their successes, they have to go on, make the lies even bigger and better. It is like an addiction. They can't help themselves."

"It sounds almost as if you've had experience with that."

Wayne shrugged. "Maybe I can identify. Not the lying bit because I try to be straightforward with people, but…wanting to be funny and have people say it's always a laugh when you are around. It's like a role you play and after a while it's just so natural that you keep doing it. Like a habit you can't break anymore."

"Even if you want to?" Erin asked with a serious look.

"I guess so." Wayne took a deep breath. "I have always seen it like this. In life you have many experiences, some good, some bad. They shape you. Under pressure you have to react in some way. And once you fall into a pattern, it is difficult to step away from that. Maybe even impossible? I don't know. I sometimes ask myself what would have happened if my mother hadn't died. Or if my father had been a more accepting man. Less demanding and controlling. Would I have grown up to be a different person? Probably. But life took those turns and I had to deal with them. Now I just have to accept that I am who I am and… It is alright."

Erin kept looking at him. A worried frown hovered over her eyes. "Is it?"

Wayne blinked. "I don't follow."

"Is it alright? That you have taught yourself a knee-jerk response? That you think showing your feelings is wrong, just because your father wouldn't allow it? That you even feel sort of…guilty for missing your mother while it is totally normal?"

Her words hit home hard. He did miss his mother and he did blame himself for that. He was a grown man, he should be over it by now, right?

Erin said, "You have taught yourself survival tactics, Wayne, to make it through that hard time in your life when you were a kid without a mother and with a father who asked too much of you. Who never made you feel like Wayne was just okay the way he was."

Wayne forced himself to look at the road and keep driving. Not stop the truck and just run away from this. He didn't want to hear it. He didn't want to realize it was true.

"You taught yourself survival tactics, because that is what you have to do. Make it through. Somehow come out on the other end." Erin's voice trembled. "But life was not meant for mere survival. It was meant to be lived. To the fullest. You have to figure out who you are and what you want and go after it. Because you owe it to yourself. You have to take back control of your own life despite the hurt you feel."

He clenched his jaw and waited for the sting behind his eyes to subside. No one had ever talked to him like that. Willing him to…break free from all the hurt of the past. It was great that she dared to say it, cared enough to say it. But at the same time he was in a panic like the horse he'd rescued. Because he didn't know how to handle this soft approach. He could deal with people's judgment and disapproval but not with someone who talked to him about how great he was. He wanted to back away and flee.

Erin said, "Maybe it doesn't sound very convincing, coming from me. Because I haven't been very good at fighting for my own freedom either. But I want to try now. I've been given a new chance. I didn't marry Hutch. I didn't accept the lies. I escaped the trap of giving in to everything he wanted. I am free to do what I want."

"And what is that?" Wayne asked, his heart sinking at what the answer might be.

Erin sighed. "I don't know. That is the thing. I know what I don't want. I don't want to ever please other people again, I want to do what is right for me. I want to truly live and…be happy. But how to do that? I feel like…other people can do it, that they know how and I don't." She wriggled her hands. "It might sound silly, but I just have no idea how to make the right decisions. My parents always decided for me until I went cruising and… That was a kind of freedom but then I fell in with Hutch and his friends, trying to please them and… Now I have to figure out who I am and what I want."

"Listen, Erin…" Wayne cast her a quick reassuring look. He felt more confident now that the spotlight had turned away from him back to her and they could discuss her life and her future. "You do know who you are and what you want. Deep inside. Just take the time to sit still and let it surface. To go back to your deepest hopes and dreams when you were a kid. To embrace what has always been living inside of you."

"Thanks for saying so, Wayne." She put her hand on his arm a moment. "You are a true friend."

Yes, that was what he wanted to be for her. A true friend. Someone she could count on now that times were difficult. Someone who would be there for her when she needed him. He wanted to spend a lot more time with her and see her smile again, laugh, be playful, or adventurous. He wanted to know much more about her. Maybe…as she got back on her feet and found her way into a new future, there would be room for him in that future too. Not just as a friend but as a romantic partner. He had no idea if she would even want that. Or if he could be a partner. Because all this closeness was nice enough but it also scared him, made him want to take a trip to a faraway place and not come back until she was gone. She shook up his world in so many ways and he didn't know what was up or down. One moment he ached to take her into his arms and hold her, the next he thought that he should keep his distance because he could only get burned.

But he had to go through this uncertainty without running. He had to give this inexplicable thing between them a chance. He sure knew that he had never felt for any woman what he felt for her. That she already took up more space in his heart than he had ever allowed anyone else. But like caring for the skittish mare, he had to be patient. She had to go through her own grief and disappointment. Make up her mind about what she wanted next. He could only walk beside her this stretch of the road. Offer her a shoulder to lean on.

And who knew what was possible for the both of them further down that road? Beyond the current horizon. If they just gave it time and hope…

CHAPTER FOURTEEN

"WHAT DO YOU THINK?" Erin stepped back and held her breath as Wayne looked at the floral display she had just finished in the entrance hall of the community center. The past five days had been spent in a flurry of preparations, meeting with people, late-night calls and early-morning messages, and today was the day on which the big anniversary celebrations were officially kicked off by the mayor. It all started in an hour. They had worked so hard to get things ready that most of the past few days felt like a haze. She had driven from one ranch to another to pick up flowers, discuss timetables, lend a hand with someone else's project who then in return helped her with hers. It had been so good to be busy and not think of Hutch, or the bills for the wedding party that were still unpaid. Wayne's lawyer friend was working on a solution so the responsibility didn't all land on her but he had told her it would take time and she just had to be patient and hope for the best.

Wayne and she had worked hard so she could create this magnificent display in the entrance hall. The number 150 was flanked by an apple tree and a horse and in the background, the Rocky Mountains. It had taken a lot of flowers from various ranchers to complete it and ensure it stayed fresh for a longer period. It was the biggest thing she had ever worked on and doubt had assailed her at times that she could not make it work. That it would be a disappointment for Wayne and the town, marring the happiness of the celebrations and making them realize they had overestimated her talent.

But as she stood here now, her heart beating heavily, she saw that it looked pretty good. She glowed inside with pride that she had created this. That she had been there for every step, from sketch design to final result, and it had turned out largely like she had pictured it in her mind. She could actually do this.

"I think it will really impress people," Wayne said. "I know they would never have imagined having something this beautiful and professional looking in their small town. They will be very grateful you happened to be here and were willing to help out."

"I'm grateful to them for entrusting me with the project." Erin looked up at Wayne. "And to you for all you did to help me, with practical stuff. Your beautiful roses." The roses he had brought her from the special bush on his ranch formed the letter *o* in Heartmont. It wasn't round like a regular *o* but shaped into a heart to emphasize the "heart" in the town's name. It had turned out so well. "And especially your moral support. At times I was certain it would so not work. At one point I was ready to throw in the towel."

"You are so talented," Wayne said, "Why would it not work?"

Erin took a deep breath, her mind coming up with a million reasons why. But then she paused. If Wayne had taught her one thing in the past few days, it was not to overthink everything. "Okay. Instead of giving you all the reasons why I think I am not as good as everybody seems to think I am, I will just embrace this compliment."

"Good," Wayne said, "because I really mean it."

She looked into his eyes. He smiled down on her with a tenderness that took her breath away. He had become so much to her in such a short span of time. He had proven to be the friend she needed but also…

Wayne leaned down gently. He closed the distance between them in slow motion, as if to give her time to pull back. Time to realize what he was going to do and figure out if she wanted it or not. But she couldn't figure out anything except that this seemed to be the place for her to be and him the man to be with and this moment just…perfect.

His lips brushed hers very gently. Like sunshine caressing her face after a cold spell the touch inserted warmth in her heart, life in her entire being. Since the morning she had seen him standing on the porch of his ranch, waiting for her, and she had felt that jolt of attraction, part of her had wanted this. Exactly this. She hadn't wanted to acknowledge it because it felt so wrong. Her wedding had barely been canceled. How could she have feelings for another man?

Even if she knew Wayne was what she had always truly wanted. Not a showboat like Hutch, but someone who was authentic. Real.

Still, was this any more real than her attraction to Hutch had been? She was only staying here for a few days to recuperate. Their lifestyles had nothing in common. Wasn't she making a major mistake again?

She gasped for breath. Her eyes widened as she stared up at him. "Wayne, no, we can't..."

He stepped back, raising a hand. "Don't say it, Erin, not today. We have a full day of festivities ahead of us. We should just enjoy them."

She could barely breathe because her heart was beating so hard. Enjoy the day? After he had done this? Kissed her like...he was attracted to her?

As she was attracted to him. She knew it with lightning strike certainty. But it was outrageous. It was totally wrong. She had wanted to marry someone else only a short while ago. Just because that guy had turned out to be a heel and a traitor, she couldn't lose herself in another man's embrace. Wayne was too good to be a bounce-back guy. To...

But she knew that he wasn't that. At all. In fact he was the one she had wanted to meet all along. His kind of support had been what she was looking for when she had fallen for Hutch. Wayne had brought her what she had always ached for. Acceptance. Trust, a boost of her self-confidence.

Wayne said softly, "I'm sorry, Erin, if you

didn't want this. But I just had to… I have felt like this…" He faltered.

She put her hand on his arm. "Don't say it, Wayne. I don't blame you for the kiss. I guess I…wanted it too. It's unbelievable maybe but it feels like I have known you so much longer than the short time I have been here. You have grown to mean so much to me that…it seems impossible such feelings can even be real. I just don't know what to think."

"Which is why we are not thinking about it. Not today anyway." He smiled down on her and brushed his hand across her cheek. "We are simply going to have a lot of fun. You deserve it for having worked so hard for this. I hope you don't feel like I ruined it all with my kiss."

"No." She shook her head and she was totally certain. "I guess I was just overtaken because…" She looked for words.

Wayne put his finger on her lips. "Later. I hear people coming."

Indeed the first volunteers poured in and soon the mayor and his wife followed. People oohed and aahed over the display and Erin had to pose with it for pictures that would be shared on social media. She also had to give an interview to a journalist for a local paper and then a TV crew from a local station came in to talk to a few people for a small item for the news. Everything went very quickly and Erin didn't have much time to think about the implications of Wayne's kiss anymore. How that one moment had shifted everything between them and made it all the more urgent that she had to decide about her future. She hadn't had much time to think about whether she wanted to go back into the real estate firm. The easy availability of the solution had its attractions. It might also be the biggest risk. What if she made another choice that wasn't really for her? That didn't reflect what she truly wanted or needed?

Now Wayne's kiss had raised more questions. What did this feeling mean? What could it mean after so short a time? And could she really settle in a small town? He was tied to his ranch and his animals. He wasn't leaving. If she wanted to be with him, she'd have to move here. Her parents would be outraged again. And did her need for bustle and excitement around her even fit with the quiet of the countryside? Was she not deceiving herself into thinking there was a real connection between Wayne and her? What about his loner mentality and his reluctance to open up to others? Was she not idolizing him, their bond, because he had helped her at the most difficult moment in her life? Emotional need wasn't a base to build her new future on.

But what was? How could she make the right decision and not regret her choices later?

WAYNE WATCHED AS Erin was being interviewed and he felt so proud of her. She had done an amazing job and today she deserved to be showered with praise. It would be good for her to realize that she was a true artist with flowers. She often doubted herself and there was no need for that.

He just wished he hadn't kissed her.

Or maybe he wished he had kissed her longer. That he had been able to convince her with the kiss to give him a chance.

Not that he wanted a chance. It was risky and wrong and…

Wayne raised a hand and rubbed his forehead. He didn't know whether to kick himself for that kiss or accept it had been inevitable. After she had been to his ranch for breakfast something inside of him had shifted and he had allowed himself to be more open to the idea they could be together. He had been hopeful that she would come to see there was something between them. For him there had been a spark of attraction ever since he had first seen her. He had not wanted to acknowledge it at that moment because she had been wearing a wedding dress. He had fully believed she was going to marry another man and he wasn't about to think about someone else's bride as a potential partner. Then she had been forced to share that the wedding was off and he had felt so sorry for her that he hadn't allowed himself to be glad that she was still free. He hadn't even consciously thought about it until later. When she had grown closer to him and he had realized that she was so much more than just a pretty woman who struck a chord inside him with her vulnerability. She was talented, funny, good-natured, kind, lending a helping hand where she could. She was everything he had ever dreamed of in a girlfriend.

But she was also off-limits. She was a city girl used to a lot more excitement than she got here. She had been super surprised Heartmont didn't have a cinema and the restaurants closed at eleven. At one point she had mentioned how she had been to museums and concert halls all over the world. How could she ever fit into a small town where winters were long and lonely without much to do except for socializing with friends at their ranches?

He didn't want her to have to make such a huge sacrifice for him. What could he offer her in return? His ramshackle ranch where there was always something to fix. His horses that he kept and tended at his own expense. His lifestyle that was far from conventional. He wasn't Alex who had been able to offer his wife a solid salary, a luxury home, nice vacations, a big car…

Not that any of this mattered. He wasn't going to ask Erin to marry him or anything. Maybe what they did, seeing so much of each other, felt a lot like dating, but the relationship would never move beyond that. She was just here for a short while, then she would leave to pursue her own dreams and ambitions. He had encouraged her to search inside herself for what she truly wanted and she was going to come up with something amazing, he just knew it. When she did, he was going to support her and that was that. He would not make it hard on her by asking her to consider a real, long-term relationship.

It was better for both of them. She was too shaken by events to see straight and make the right decision and he was…well, he didn't know what he was, but he felt differently than he ever had before and it was…uncomfortable to say the least. Unnerving, scary, risky…what didn't cover it?

Erin said goodbye to the crew and came over to him. There was a high color in her cheeks. "I hope I didn't ramble. I didn't have much time to prepare. They asked me questions about Heartmont and I had to admit I am not a native."

You hear that? She is not a native. Not one of you. "I'm sure you did fine. You pick up new things quickly."

She beamed at him. "They said the floral display was amazing. Coming from them it must be true. I mean, they often see such displays at other events they cover and they can compare, you know?"

He nodded. "I understand. Hey, how about a cup of coffee? You haven't had anything for hours. We could go across the street and have a donut too."

"Great idea." She fell into step beside him. "I am so happy for today. That the people of Heartmont will feel like their little town is celebrated in a memorable way. A hundred and fifty years is amazing. It means there is so much history here and so much heart blood. I mean, the investment of so many people to make this a community. Their belief in it, their hopes and dreams, it is like I can almost feel it." She fell silent and flushed even deeper. "Maybe you think that is weird."

"No, I do understand what you mean. We all have a connection with the past, with the generations who came before us and who built this town." They were outside now and he gestured around him to the shops, the diner and the church further down the street. The businesses all had black-and-white photographs in their windows of how the street had looked through the decades as Heartmont had developed, and their entrances were decorated with golden balloons. The diner advertised a special anniversary menu and at the church several local choirs were performing through the day. "They built it with love. They put a little something of themselves into everything they created here. The blacksmith, the carpenter, the plumber, the glass blower… They all left their stamp on the buildings and the streets. Maybe that is why I wanted to keep on living here, even when my brother left and my father followed him. Because I feel connected to the history of the people who were here before me. Because I want to follow in their footsteps and tend the land and…"

Erin smiled at him. "I think you are all very lucky to have such a beautiful heritage here."

"Erin!" A female voice resounded to their left. Erin turned her head to look in that direction. He could feel her freeze when she saw who was coming over to them. Dressed in a linen pantsuit with an expensive bag on her arm and towering heels, Livia Lakewood drew closer. She beamed at Erin as she spread out her arms. "How are you?" She leaned in and kissed Erin.

Erin seemed rooted to the spot. She fumbled, "Livia… What are you doing here? When I messaged you three days ago, you said you were in New York City party planning."

"I was. I flew back here last night. You mentioned how the town was celebrating its anniversary today. That you have been involved. I thought I would come over and have a look. This is all so cute." Livia looked around her. "Really sweet and full of country charm."

Erin seemed to cringe under her assessment, grow smaller as she stood there barely looking at her sister. Wayne wished that Livia would not take this high-handed approach. She might mean well, but it was obvious that she herself felt no connection to a country lifestyle or small-town ways.

Erin said, "Livia, I'm of course happy to see you and you are most welcome to join in the town celebrations, but...you can't have finished the job in NYC already."

"I'm multitasking." Livia made a gesture as if it was all small stuff. "Some time back I was asked by a tech mogul to check out some possibilities for him and his family to party here in the fall. I scouted locations online and I thought I might as well come to see them in person and then drop by Heartmont for an hour or so to say hi to you." She hesitated a moment and added, "I do want you to know I appreciate that you reached out first with your messages and that I carry no grudge for what happened."

Wayne felt his jaw drop. Erin had been upset after Livia accused her of billing the firm on her first visit, but she had wanted to build bridges and he had encouraged her to do so. The text message exchange had seemed to go well and Erin had been hopeful she could repair the bond with her family. Now Livia had galloped back into town to look down on all they had arranged for here and then tell Erin she carried no grudge? As if Erin was the culprit!

His intentions to help Erin patch things up with her family seemed to evaporate under his rising irritation over Livia's way of handling things. He didn't need someone to come and make Erin feel that Heartmont was beneath her. Especially when he had hoped that she would feel more connected to it. To him. To them.

Livia said, "What a darling little coffee shop on the other side of the street. Shall we have a coffee there and something sweet? I really want to talk to you. About something important." She flashed Wayne a pearly smile. "I'm sorry to be dragging Erin away, but I just want to talk to her one on one, for a few minutes. Then she will be all yours again to uh...carry on with the celebrations or whatever you have planned for the day."

Her tone made it clear that whatever it was it couldn't amount to much in her book. Wayne wanted to say that he wasn't letting Erin go with her, not even for a few minutes. Who did Livia Lakewood think she was, just breezing in here and taking charge? He wished Erin had never messaged her and told her about the anniversary celebrations she was a part of.

But Erin said, "Maybe it's better if I do talk to Livia, Wayne. It won't take long. I'll come and find you later. Okay?" She cast him a pleading look. How could he say no? Even if he thought it was a bad idea. Because he knew, better than most people, how difficult family relations could be. And how much you wanted to fit in, even against your own better judgment.

"Okay," he said and watched the two sisters cross the street for the coffee cafe. He had a sinking feeling he was letting Erin walk straight into some kind of trap. Livia might have business around the area but that didn't exclude an ulterior motive in showing up here. A hidden agenda to get Erin back on track toward the future Livia wanted for her. He had heard enough about the family dynamics to realize that Erin had always been under the influence of her older sister. But there was nothing he could do to protect her now.

CHAPTER FIFTEEN

ERIN'S HEART BEAT like a drum as she accompanied her smartly dressed sister across the street. She felt like she had always felt beside Livia: inadequate. Somehow smaller than she really was. Underdressed. Not qualified. The compliments she had received for her floral display faded to the back of her mind and all she could see was how she didn't fit in here and it was just silly she had decided to stay here after Hutch had deceived her.

Something Livia didn't even know about!

Livia said, "You have really done a nice job here to celebrate the town anniversary. I suppose it is a major event when not much else happens."

"These people feel connected to a past, a history they share. A heritage. It is more important than you can ever imagine."

Livia blinked. For a moment she seemed to want to flare, then she said in a friendlier voice, "I'm sorry. I didn't know you felt that involved. It is like you though to dive into anything you do, feel such a personal commitment. I am more businesslike in that respect. I want to do a good job, for sure, but I try to keep it professional and stay emotionally unattached."

Erin wanted to ask if Livia had ever felt emotionally attached to anything or anyone in her life. But that would be unnecessarily rude and unkind. Livia was who she was. Her zeal and dedication had taken her a long way. She was a super successful businesswoman and Erin did admire her for that. She could only hope Livia would also try to see Erin's values and respect those.

They went inside the coffee shop and claimed the last free table against the far wall. A waitress breezed by taking their order and then Livia leaned across the table and said, "I am so glad I caught you. I know I should have let you know that I was coming but… I thought a surprise would be more fun."

Erin didn't comment. Livia probably meant a surprise attack. She wanted something, obviously, and Erin was afraid to think what it might be.

"Since you are involved in the celebrations, I knew you would be here so I arranged for

Mom and Dad to come as well. I wanted to bring the parties together to uh…smooth things over. You know, have a reunion of sorts? They are right now looking inside some kind of museum…" Her lips pursed as if she could barely force herself to call it a museum. "They don't need to be here while I speak with you and update you on the situation. I'm happy to report they took it really well when I said I had heard via the grapevine that your relationship with Hutch had ended."

Erin's jaw slackened. She had never reckoned Livia would share that news with their parents first. She had fully counted on her sister wanting Erin to do this herself. After all, it was her life they were talking about. Why did Livia always have to treat her like a little child?

"I emphasized that the breakup had been your decision. They were really relieved and glad you came to your senses. He never fitted into our family and would just have hurt your interests. Now that you've seen the light and acted on your new insights, we can move on."

Erin was too stunned to ask what she meant by moving on. Her brain had stopped working at the realization her parents knew about the breakup. She'd have to face them soon, knowing that they might find out the entire truth at some point.

Livia sat up straighter and folded her hands on the table. “Mom and Dad know nothing about that unfortunate bill Hutch dropped on us, or about the wedding you didn’t invite us to. I suggest it will be our little secret. I’m willing to cover for you if you just…don’t cause any more drama. I mean… Mom and Dad really need to have the family reunited again.”

Erin didn’t know if it was smart to agree to this. Lies were bound to come out and once they did, Mom and Dad would blame her, not Livia, who had suggested this plan.

Livia said almost under her breath, “They missed you.”

Erin stared at her sister. She saw how hard it was for Livia to say this. To acknowledge that her presence as the successful eldest daughter hadn’t been enough. That their parents had still missed the runaway. The prodigal daughter. The one who had never wanted to be part of the family firm.

“They need you,” Livia said. Her voice was brittle and she clenched her neatly manicured hands together. “They never said so to my face but I overheard a conversation…”

She took a deep breath as if she had to steel

herself against what she had learned, unwittingly. "They want you in the firm. They have invested so much time and energy into that business. You know how it was when we were little. We barely saw them. They did it all for us, to have something to offer to us. Now we must repay them with respect and…commitment. I know how once you decide to do something you stick with it. You are loyal. I have often seen it. Outside the firm. For other people's ventures. Now you need to consider laying it all on the line for family. It would make them so happy."

Livia waited a moment and added, her features tense, "I realize I can't give it to them without you, Erin. They want us both to be part of what they built. They want to do this as a family, standing together. Please come back?"

Erin sat motionless. Livia would never have been able to convince her with loud arguments or a list of the financial benefits, or accusations and reproaches. But this forced admission that she could not help her parents be completely happy and that she needed Erin for that, really hit home. What kind of daughter would Erin be if she didn't want her parents to be happy? Had she not always craved her parents' love? Their recognition of her talents and her value for the family business? Now it seemed she could have all that. If she just accepted their offer to come back home.

Also for Livia's sake. This was one of the rare occasions where she had said please to Erin. Where she actually needed her. And Erin could blame Livia all she wanted for being more successful and making her feel bad about herself, but she also still cared for Livia. They were sisters after all. They had also had good times. They shared a family legacy, an unbreakable bond.

Livia said, "Dad will tell you all about his plans later. I should have probably not run ahead and told you all this. He should never know that I did. But I wanted to make sure… I know you a little, Erin. You can be stubborn, not willing to take an outstretched hand. But Dad is not doing this to lean in and support you. He is doing this for himself and Mom. You should try and…forget about the past to make it better for them. They so deserve that after all the hard work they put into the business. The success they have is not enough. They need the family to stand together. Would you consider it? Could you?"

Livia's voice was pleading now. Erin felt her eyelids burn. She reached out and took her sister's hand in hers. "I will do my very best, Livia, to be open to Dad's offer. I know how hard it must have been for you to come here and tell me all of this."

Livia took another deep breath. "I had to do it. I was afraid you would think that...nobody needs you. But it has never been like that. Mom and Dad always wanted you in the firm. Maybe even more than me. You are the creative one, you always have all the good ideas."

"That is not true. They value you a lot for your business acumen, your practical approach."

Livia suppressed a bleak smile. "Let's stop killing each other with kindness, okay? I know it will be hard to work together again. We have all had our expectations go awry. But we are still family. We owe it to each other to give it a try. At least, I know I want to try."

"I do want to try as well," Erin said, squeezing her sister's hand. The waitress arrived with their coffees and donuts and Livia pulled back, visibly embarrassed to be caught like this. She cleared her throat as the waitress put the order on the table. As soon as the woman had removed herself, Livia said, "That is a deal then. I will meet Mom and Dad in an hour and pretend I have been scouting for my next party.

They need never know we met." She laughed shakily. "I am glad that we did, you know. I feel much better now." She looked at the donut with the pink glazing. "This looks nice."

Erin nodded. As she picked up her coffee, she realized with a shock what she had just done. Caught up in the emotion of the moment, the reunion with her sister and Livia's unexpected vulnerability, she had not thought through the consequences of her decision. That to promise to consider Dad's offer to come back into the firm she was also moving away from Heartmont, from all she had found here. From Wayne.

He had kissed her. He had totally confused her. What kind of woman was she, having just walked away from the wedding to the man she had called the love of her life and now having feelings for someone else? It made her so uncomfortable that solely for that reason she wanted to run. But there was more. Wayne came closer to her ideal man than Hutch ever had. With Hutch she had always tried to be the savvy woman he wanted her to be. With Wayne she didn't have to pretend. She could be herself and still he was falling for her, still…

It was so confusing. She didn't understand any of it. He had seen her at her lowest and still he cared for her? How was that possible? Was it pity? Was it sympathy? Or was it his tendency to reach out and help anyone who'd lost their way? Maybe she was like that scared horse he tended. Was it really even about her?

She didn't know. She needed time to work it all out, to make the situation clearer to herself. But would she have enough time now that Livia had popped up and her parents too? In an hour they would be here, smiling at her, showing their approval of her decision to break it off with Hutch. She felt like she didn't deserve that appreciation since they didn't know the full truth. Livia had called it their little secret. But was this wise? What was she getting into?

There was panic inside of her. Her family had always expected things of her she couldn't deliver. Was rejoining the firm not a recipe for disaster? At the same time she wanted to please them and show them and herself that she could be the daughter they wanted.

The daughter they had missed.

Livia had not lied about that. It had cost her to admit it. She had been almost disappointed about it. Which was logical as Livia had of course tried to fill the void and be everything her parents needed and wanted. But it had been impossible for her to fill Erin's place. Wasn't that amazing? That she had been missed? That they wanted her back because they needed her?

It was more than she had dared to hope earlier. It was like an unexpected gift. Why not take it, embrace it?

What else would she do?

Erin sipped her coffee and smiled at Livia who praised the donut anew. It felt uncomfortable to sit here and have nothing essential to discuss. To sense how hard even small talk seemed. But they had been alienated for a while and needed to feel their way back to each other. It could be done. If she wanted it enough. Livia wanted it. Mom and Dad wanted it. Now all she had to do was want it as well. She could do it. She had to. For them, for herself, to prove a point. To show everyone that she wasn't a loser. Not someone who gave up and walked away. No, someone who could build bridges and make their family work again.

Yes. She owed it to everyone to give this a try. She didn't want to think about Wayne at this moment. About how he might feel when he heard her news. It was complicated enough as it was. She had to meet her parents first and see how that worked out. How it felt, what they had to say. If they could find some common ground.

Her palms were sweaty just thinking about it. She had doubted her abilities to make the anniversary floral decorations work. This morning, seeing how it had all turned out, she had felt better about herself and wished she hadn't ruined her joy by all that second-guessing. But now the questions raged through her head again and she didn't feel up to the challenge. She actually wished Wayne was here to tell her that she could do it.

But would he tell her that, if he knew that her reunion with her parents would take her away from him? It seemed she was approaching a fork in the road, an intersection where choices would have to be made. And what would she do then? Which direction would she take, and what would it mean for her future?

HALF AN HOUR LATER, still a little weak in the knees after all the excitement, Erin stood in the middle of a crowd cheering for the parade that passed through Heartmont's town center. There were old-timer cars and all kinds of agricultural vehicles. Wayne, who stood beside her, tried to shout some explanations in her ear but the sounds created by the long line of vehicles and the roars of the spectators drowned out most of what he said. She did appreciate that he was trying to make her a part of this.

But even though she didn't catch what he said, she felt like she belonged here by his side. They had worked hard for this day and now it was finally here and everybody was enjoying themselves. They ought to be proud.

She reached out to touch his arm and as he looked down on her, she shouted, "You did a great job for all of this."

"What?" He leaned over to her and yelled, "I can't make out what you said."

"You did a great..." She realized it was futile and had to laugh. "Never mind, I'll tell you later."

He smiled at her before looking at the parade again. It was good to stand here with him, like they were sort of...a couple? As if they were dating?

What was she thinking? Okay, they were attracted to each other, and they had become emotionally close in a way she had never experienced with anyone else before, but their lives were worlds apart. She liked what she saw here, but that didn't mean that she could suddenly fit in. People led completely different lives here, in tune with the seasons, working the land and forming a true community.

They had deep personal connections and loyalty beyond what she was used to in the city. There socializing had often been work related, like Dad's golf tournaments which he used to network, or Mom's client events. Socializing was like performing to expectations, playing a role in a larger whole. But these people *were* the town. They formed the beating heart of it. When there was a problem, they all felt it as if it was their very own problem. When they raised money, they put their hearts and souls into it, because it benefited their own elderly or children or farmers' community. She had never quite experienced anything like it before. And it felt so special.

But she was a stranger, having landed here by chance. By some mishap in her own life that had catapulted her into Wayne's. He had been gracious about it, picking her up and dusting her off, but it wasn't like she was suddenly one of them. She was an outsider, looking in on their festivities. It was nice enough, but she had to keep reminding herself that usually this small town was a lot quieter than the city she was used to or life on a cruise ship. So many things she enjoyed were missing here. No cinemas, no fancy restaurants, no indoor climbing center or large sports facilities, no delis where she could buy exotic fruits and spices to cook with. No pottery classes, no art museum. Everything here was centered on the country lifestyle, and if you grew up with it, you might not miss the things city life could offer. But she had always had that experience, a blend of excitement and adventure, especially when she had been traveling on the cruise ship. Regardless of whether she'd go back into the business with Mom and Dad, she did picture her future somewhere else than in the middle of nowhere. She had to remind herself of that, over and over. In case her heart was foolish enough to start whispering something else…

The last old tractor chugged past them and the hubbub around them died down a bit. Wayne said, "You were saying?"

"You should be very proud of yourself for what you created here. You and the entire committee. I'm sure the tourists are super enjoying it."

"And you?" he asked. "Are you enjoying it?" The answer seemed to matter a lot to him, judging by the look in his eyes.

"I'm having a wonderful day." *For one summer day this is nice enough. But could it be my life every day? What would it be like in winter, when it must be cold and gray and dreary and there is so little to do?* She took a deep breath. She had to tell Wayne about her conversation with Livia at some point and now was as good a time as any. "Not in the least because Livia showed up and extended an olive branch to me."

WAYNE FROZE AT the mention of Livia's name. He wasn't happy at all that the big sister had descended on the town again. He had a sinking feeling it had something to do with taking Erin away from here and putting her firmly back in the family fold. He wasn't sure that was really what Erin wanted or needed, but who was he to disagree? Besides, Erin wasn't asking for his opinion.

He nodded. "I hope you can patch things up. I mean, it's never nice when family relations are under pressure. And now that you broke up with the man they didn't want for you, I suppose there is every reason to reconnect."

Erin grimaced. "It does feel like they are telling me: now that you measure up to our ideals again, you are welcome to come back."

Come back. Did that also mean come back home? Would she be leaving soon?

At the idea a painful void opened in his stomach. He had just found her. He was barely starting to open up to the idea of getting close to someone. He had kissed her and he wanted to do that again. Why had Livia come? Today of all days? This was supposed to have been their day, to spend together and see what was possible.

But he fought the disappointment and kept eyeing her with what he hoped was friendly interest. "They might never admit that they missed you."

"In fact, Livia did say Mom and Dad missed me. That she could not make up for my absence. I had honestly never expected her to say something like that. I felt very touched and… also kind of relieved. Because I always thought they were better off without me."

Like Wayne often thought about Dad and Alex. Better off without Wayne, who had never made the grade. He was glad Erin no longer had to think that. Because it hurt. "See?" he said. "Things are very different from what you thought. I'm glad for you." It felt like he had to betray everything inside of him to say those words.

But he had to say them. For her sake.

"Mom and Dad are coming over to meet me. I'm kind of nervous about it. Is that odd to be nervous about meeting your own parents?"

"I guess that for most people it would be odd. Because they have a bond where they don't feel like they..." Have to perform? Prove something? "Where they can just be themselves. But at this moment in time you're not completely sure of where you stand so it's logical to feel nervous. Still, it will be alright, I'm sure."

"Thanks, Wayne, you really cheer me up." Erin smiled at him. "I hope you don't feel like I'm walking out on you to meet my parents. It will only be for a little while. Then I'll be back to have some of the delicious food with you and of course we have to see the fireworks together."

"Of course," he agreed but an uneasy feeling came over him. How would she come back to him? As a changed person? Because her parents had hugged her and told her that they wanted her back home now that the unwanted fiancé had disappeared? Now that the marriage was off the cards?

He knew all too well how persuasive people could be. How manipulative also. With the best intentions of course. No doubt Erin's parents thought that they were really doing their daughter a favor. But still... Was this right for Erin? Was it what she needed in her life right now?

He wasn't sure. He didn't know her all that

well. He felt like he did, because they had shared hard stuff, emotional moments. But wasn't it more logical that people who had known her all her life knew what was best for her? What fitted her character, her lifestyle?

He couldn't deny she was a city girl who had landed in a ranching community. She had adjusted quickly and worked with them like a pro to get everything organized for this big day, but that only testified to her professional expertise. It didn't mean that she felt a personal connection with their way of life. It didn't mean that she…would ever want to come back here or stay in touch with him or… He didn't even want to think further than that. Dad had lectured him enough about the disadvantages of small-town life to know that Erin would have to give up a lot of things to ever come and live in the country. To consider it, there would have to be a strong draw here.

Erin said, "Oh, I see Mom and Dad on the other side of the street. Livia said they'd be at the diner around noon, but I guess they came a little early. I'll go and meet them right now. See you later." He watched as she hurried away, rushed to meet her folks. Her steps were light, and it didn't seem she was worried or fearful at all. But outer appearances could be deceiving. How could he know what she was really thinking?

Still he stood and watched the meeting as if what he saw could reveal something important to him. Something he needed to know.

Her father was a nice-looking tall man who put an arm around his daughter at once. And her mother, a little shorter with her blond hair drawn back in a sporty ponytail, immediately leaned in to kiss Erin on the cheek. When a stranger observed this scene, he would conclude these people were close and loved each other very much.

Which was probably true. Her parents loved her and only wanted the best for her. Which of course had to do with money and status and having the good life with all the expensive holidays and opportunities. Wayne could understand that. The lifestyle might not work for him personally, but he did understand that others craved it and thought it was the highest form of happiness. Erin came from that world. She had always lived in it, first with her parents and sister, then as she cruised the world. That was a luxury lifestyle too, even if you were a member of the crew. It was all about travel and broadening your horizons. Not about being stuck in one place where all you ever did was scrape manure off your boots. Quote, unquote, his father.

Wayne took a deep breath and tried to shed the tension that crawled across his back straight into his shoulders and neck. He couldn't change a thing about this situation. Erin was meeting her parents and they wanted to make up with her, which was in itself wonderful for her. What it might mean for him, for them…

Them? There was no them. Yes, they had kissed, but they had both concluded that had been a mistake. That it wasn't right. No matter how right it had felt.

He turned away abruptly. He couldn't just stand there and stare at her as she was moving away from his life. He had to go and do something. He would hear later what her parents had said and how she had responded to it.

CHAPTER SIXTEEN

Erin smiled at her mother who was going on about how nice the town looked and how friendly everyone had been pointing them in the right direction when they had been a little lost getting here. "It really is the middle of nowhere," she concluded with a raised eyebrow. "I still don't understand how you ended up here for a job."

"But..." her father rushed to say, "you did great. We saw your interview on the news."

"Oh yes," Mom enthused now. "The flowers at the community center looked amazing. Especially the roses in that cute heart in the name Heartmont."

The roses. Wayne's roses. Her heart made a little jump when she thought of him. His flowers were amazing and he was amazing. She wanted to kiss him again. The thought came unbidden and at an awkward moment when she was trying to appease her parents after the very difficult time in their relationship. But it was true. She wanted to kiss Wayne again. She wanted to spend time with him. In fact, this meeting felt like an unwelcome disruption. Intrusion on her personal enjoyment of the day she had worked hard for.

She flushed at her own thoughts. How ungrateful when her parents had made time for her, had no doubt canceled other engagements to be here. To meet the daughter who had slighted them. She said quickly, "I'm so happy you are here. Livia had already told me you were coming and… I…" She wanted to say, *I missed you* but felt she couldn't without crying. It reminded her so much of the unpleasant cold hours preparing for her wedding, knowing her family hadn't been invited and it was all her fault. That she was doing the wrong thing and still she hadn't known how to do it any other way.

Dad said, "Let's have lunch, shall we? There must be some place here where they serve a good salad with a nice glass of white wine? I don't expect anything grand, not in a place like this, but…one must make do."

"Yes, let's have lunch and discuss things," Mom said with a happy little smile. She took Erin's arm and ushered her along. "We are so pleased that you stopped cruising. That you want to do more floral work on solid ground again. And we have a wonderful idea."

"We better wait until we sit with our wine," Dad warned from behind them.

Erin almost had to laugh. This was the way their parents operated. Mom was always moving ahead quickly trying to seal the deal in a heartbeat while Dad wanted to create atmosphere and waited for the right moment to strike. It was kind of endearing to find they hadn't changed at all. It was like old times and...she could go right back to them?

She had felt so special when Livia had told her how she had been missed. She had acknowledged she had also missed them. It was like the words had opened a door to a future she had considered a closed book. Now it was possible again.

Mom said, "Erin, dearest, you just... I wish you could..." She fell silent and when Erin glanced at her mother's face, she saw the sadness there in a flash, in the lines around her mouth and the way she batted her lashes too fast. Like she had to blink back tears?

"I do hope," Erin said quickly to make it easier on her, "that you are not angry at me for how I acted when you tried to show me what

Hutch was all about. I wanted to see his good side and… It was all my fault."

"Oh no, we're only grateful that it was your own decision. You see, it is never a good idea when you have to force someone to do something they don't agree with. It can only lead to trouble. Arguments and reproaches. Now you've had time to figure it out for yourself and… I just hope you are not too disappointed?" She pressed Erin's arm.

"It was a hard decision to make," Erin said truthfully, "but once I had made it, I knew it was the right one. There was no doubt left in my mind."

"Great. That is just wonderful. Then we can forget about this whole thing." They had come to a few outdoor tables with checkered cloths and Dad said they could sit right here and have a glass of wine. He flagged down a waiter and ordered. His somewhat superior tone made Erin cringe a bit. But she did love them. They meant well.

Once they were seated in the sun, Dad leaned back and said, "Erin, you have to come back into the business. You have a flair for decorating places. Besides, Livia is doing more party planning these days and…we need the extra hands. I know I can't say this in a fancy way to convince you, or that offering you a company car and a bag of money might not convince you either, but…"

"I would like to know," Erin said, with a catch in her voice, "that I can really contribute. Bring something someone else can't."

Her mother said, "Did you ever doubt that, darling?"

Erin hung her head.

It was silent except for a bird singing in the distance. Then her mother said, "You did doubt that." There was shock in her voice. "Darling, why? We have always shown you we love you. We gave you everything you needed. The best education, birthday parties, we paid for every hobby you wanted to try…"

"Yes," her father added, "and once you worked for us, you got a regular pay raise and…"

"I just guess I wanted to hear that I was doing a good job," Erin said softly. She glanced at her father. "To know that I am a part of the firm not just because I am your daughter, but because you believe that I am the best person for the job."

"You are." Dad held her gaze. "You are our daughter and because of that, you deserve to be in our firm. You deserve to be our right hand whenever we take new actions. But you are also incredibly talented and we wouldn't want to work with anybody else."

Erin let the words flow over her, land inside of her. Dad was sparse with compliments because he himself had this *you just do your job, your duty* attitude. But now this…

It meant so much to her.

"I couldn't have put it better," Mom said, resting her hand on Erin's. "We want you back because we…need you."

Erin felt tears in her eyes. She had so longed for a conversation like this when she was still working in the company. She had longed for it after she had left to go cruising. That they would admit she had been valuable and that they wanted her back.

Over time it had seemed it would never happen. And especially after she had started dating Hutch and they had turned against the relationship, it had seemed a given that they would be detached, distant, forever.

Now they sat here and suddenly everything was alright again. She was back in their good graces. No, it was more than that. She knew they had always cared. Even if they had never said so, they had cared.

She swallowed hard. "This means so much to me."

"We wish we had said it sooner," Mom said. She squeezed Erin's hand. "We were just...concerned about your relationship with that unsuitable man. We were too busy trying to wean you away from him to realize we were losing you and...we are sorry."

"He is gone now," Dad said brusquely. "No need to discuss him anymore."

The waiter arrived and put glasses of white wine on the table. Dad picked his up and toasted her. "To your return to the firm."

Mom followed his example.

Erin felt the happiness, the giddiness of this moment of reconciliation rush through her veins. She picked up her own glass and touched it to theirs. "To our family."

"To being back together," Mom said and winked at her.

THE BIG ANNIVERSARY barbeque began around four in the afternoon. Long tables held all the different dishes locals had prepared. Men in leather aprons were grilling the meat. Delicious scents hung in the air and lured even more people. Wayne hadn't seen Erin again since she had left to meet with her parents. She had said it would just be a brief meeting but apparently they had other ideas. He had texted her around two to ask where she was, but she had not replied. Part of him was suddenly fearful she had left with her parents. That they had simply demanded her to pack her things and go with them straightaway.

Without really looking what he was doing he loaded his plate with burgers and salad. It hurt to think she would not keep her promise to join him for the food and the fireworks. But he had no idea how persuasive her parents could be. Or how much Erin herself simply wanted to feel loved. Couldn't he understand that?

"Hey. You must be hungry." Her voice touched him like a caress on his cheek. Suddenly she was there by his side, smiling up at him. He looked at her as if he saw her for the very first time. She was so beautiful. Her face beamed with happiness. To see him?

His heart responded by speeding up and he couldn't keep a mega grin from appearing on his face. "I uh… I don't want all this food but I was distracted."

"Really?" She took a plate from a stack and selected a burger. "I hope I didn't miss too much? Once my father gets to talking about his favorite topics, he simply doesn't stop. I had to look at photos of all his golf tournaments and a little presentation of the resort in the Bahamas he bought shares in."

Wayne nodded as if he was also used to conversing about golf and shares on a daily basis. But the realization how different they really were poured cold water on his happiness at being with her again. Even if she wasn't totally caught up in life in the fast lane like her parents obviously were, she would probably want a little more than to just sit around a small town doing a floral arrangement for the community center. She also deserved more. A career that took her places and gave her the recognition she craved.

Erin said, "I'm sorry it took so long. I had meant to get back to you much sooner. But I also know Mom and Dad canceled other plans to be here today and meet me and it seemed a little rude to just walk away after half an hour."

She didn't need to walk away after half an hour but to his mind she also didn't need to stay with them for almost four hours without contacting him. He had a sinking feeling that once she was with them, she wanted to please them and her own wishes had to take a back seat to theirs. In his opinion that did not make for a very healthy relationship. "You don't have to feel obliged to explain to me. I can understand you hadn't seen them for a while and you had some catching up to do. I just hope it was all…friendly?"

Erin nodded with a happy smile. "Very friendly. Now that they know Hutch is out of the way, they are pleased. I guess I can't blame them either. He wasn't good for me." She took her time adding some tomatoes and olives to her plate before saying, "Dad wants me to get back into the firm."

Ice settled into Wayne's stomach. He felt very silly standing there with that plate full of food which he could no longer eat. He had to swallow before he could ask, "And? What did you say?"

"I didn't get much of a chance to say anything. Dad already had the wine out to toast to our reunion and our future successes. That is how they usually operate. Take the ground quickly." She said it with an affectionate tone in her voice, not like she was offended by their approach. "I guess I should be happy they are not angry that I abandoned them earlier when I took up a career in cruising. Of course I quit that to marry Hutch so… Which they don't know. Just that I quit. They think I got tired of it, or wanted a little more than working to give others a pleasant vacation. They never thought cruising was a real option for me anyway."

"And how did you feel?"

Erin sighed. "It was a way to get away from home and do something with flowers. It was not like a big career wish I had cherished since third grade."

She studied the bowl with pineapple for a moment, deep in thought. Then she said, "Now they want me back in the family company. Also because Livia is doing more party planning and they are short a pair of hands. Capable hands." She looked at him. "My father actually told me that he thought I was capable. That is a big deal. I don't want to come back because I am their daughter, but because they actually feel I can do a good job."

"I can relate. My father would probably never say that to me."

Erin selected some cottage cheese and bread and then turned away from the long table. "Shall we find a place to sit? A little privacy would be nice."

"Come on, I know just the place." He led her away from the crowd who were seated at long tables eating and laughing and talking. They went around a corner, then through a narrow archway into a yard. The volunteers who worked on the preparations had often eaten lunch here. But now it was deserted as everyone was gathered round the barbeque area. Wayne gestured for her to sit on one of the white folding chairs.

Erin sat down and balanced her plate on her knees. "I can't believe he made me that offer. Or that he was so warm to me. I mean, my father is never rude or mean. He is always very polite and correct in what he says. But this time I felt like…he was being sincere about it. That he wasn't telling me things I wanted to hear, but…he meant it all. I just can't…" She used her fork to shuffle through her olives. "I guess it is just strange to know that they actually missed me while I was away. In my mind they were continuing without me and it was all just fine because I had never fitted in there to begin with. Now I have to rethink everything."

Wayne nodded. He cut off a piece of burger and stuffed it into his mouth. He could pretend he was too busy eating to say much. Because he wanted to say things to keep her from rejoining the family firm and he didn't know if he was even allowed to.

He had noticed before that Erin was insecure about herself. Something completely unnecessary because she was talented and wonderful in all she did. But she didn't believe it. He didn't know how he could make her believe it. But maybe this sudden offer could help her along. Maybe her parents' praise and acceptance would get her on track believing in herself and her abilities. He so wanted that for her. Because of all she was.

Erin said, "I guess I need to sleep on it and then in the morning I will know it is right. I'm pretty sure I'll wake up feeling ready to go with them."

"With them? Tomorrow?" Panic rushed through Wayne. She was thinking about leaving! Tomorrow! His mind balked at the mere idea. She couldn't leave so soon. They had barely had a chance to do fun things together. He wanted to show her so much more.

"Dad wants me to come with them and… well, I didn't know what to say to decline. The job here on the floral displays for the anniversary is completed and…"

"Today is just the kickoff for the celebrations. Your work here need not be done yet." He said it quickly, knowing it sounded weak. Reaching for reasons, he added, "I thought you also liked reconnecting with April? Besides, my lawyer friend is still looking into your bills."

"I know and I'm in no hurry to leave, but

I guess I feel a little obliged to do what they want. Because they extended this nice offer to me and… I haven't been completely truthful about Hutch and me. They know I broke up with him but not under what circumstances. Or that I was about to marry him without them present. I guess I want to leave with them, quickly, to prevent them from finding out what happened. The resort is close to this place and… I just don't want to linger near unhappy memories, you see?"

"I totally understand." Wayne clenched his knife and fork. She saw Heartmont as a place of unhappy memories. Because it was close to here that her no-good fiancé had betrayed her and she had run off in her wedding dress, with a broken heart. She had happened to meet him and he had taken her away from the resort, but not far away enough. She wanted to rush back to her old life, with her parents and the belief she could do a great job working for them.

That was something good, he supposed. That she had a plan and a way to restart her life after the big disappointment. It was always good to work hard. Try and forget. But he would not easily forget her.

Maybe he would never forget her?

Because Erin had touched his life in ways

no one else ever had. He had suddenly seen a way to get close to someone else. To open up and not feel vulnerable. In conversations she hadn't pushed him to share, no, he had actually wanted to do so. That was strange and new and…fantastic. But the feeling wouldn't get the chance to grow.

Erin said, "Anyway, I don't need to think about it now. I just want to have fun. Enjoy the day. We worked hard for it." She chewed a few moments and then said, "You are not angry with me, are you, Wayne? Not just for disappearing for a few hours because my parents came to town, but also…" She took a deep breath and then eyed him. "Am I making a mistake? By wanting to go with them tomorrow?"

Wayne stared into her eyes. He could lose himself in those eyes. In her smile, in the vulnerability he saw there. He wanted to look at her and just forget about having to answer that question. What could he say anyway? He wasn't an impartial bystander. He had a stake in all of this. A huge stake.

"I could use a friend's opinion." Erin's voice was soft, coaxing.

A friend, she called him. That was good, he supposed. At least they were more than just passersby. They were friends. But he wanted to be so much more to her. He wanted to sweep her into his arms and hold her and kiss her and tell her he needed her and she shouldn't leave. She should stay here with him. Always.

"I think it's a good idea to go with them." He heard himself say the words and he even sounded cool and collected, convincing. "You need something to do to take your mind off the debacle with Hutch and you can at the same time rebuild your bond with your parents. They have obviously conquered their own pride or maybe even fear of rejection to come to you and talk honestly about what happened. That is huge. My father would never do something like that. That is only weakness in his book. But your parents didn't think of themselves or their opinions when they came here. They knew they had to reach out to you and they did that. I admire them for that."

"Me too. I think it is amazing. I had never expected it. Had someone told me they would do that, I wouldn't have believed it either." She smiled softly. "It's so special."

"You should go with them and work on great floral displays in all the homes they sell. You will be able to put all of your creativity into that and...they will see you are even better than they thought."

Erin put her plate away and said, "Oh Wayne, thank you for all you say and do and…for who you are." She threw her arms around his neck and hugged him.

He held onto his plate with one hand to make sure it didn't drop to the ground. That hand was his hold on reality.

His other hand landed on her lower back and it was like touching the forbidden. The future of love he ached for, but couldn't see for himself. He wasn't right for her. She needed someone uncomplicated. Not someone with baggage and moods. She needed someone with money and status to satisfy her parents. They had only just forgiven her for having gone with Hutch. She could hardly disappoint them again by choosing him.

And there was no choice involved anyway. She was thinking about leaving. She hadn't said there was anything that might keep her here. Had a hold on her heart, or whatever.

It was all over.

He had to remind himself of that.

It was all over.

ERIN BURIED HER face against Wayne's shoulder. She breathed the scent of his aftershave, of horses and leather, of all that was Wayne.

Her heart was light because of the reconciliation with her parents, the appreciation she suddenly got from them that was like a balm to her bruised heart. But in these moments hugging Wayne she also felt pain shoot through her that she was saying goodbye to him, to Heartmont, to all she had found here. This town had been so good to her. Had shown her she was someone worthwhile even after she had lost everything. She had come here with no job, no home, no partner. Nothing. And still people had welcomed her and cared for her and offered her chances. They had believed in her when she herself couldn't. It had helped her through very hard times and pushed her forward toward a better future.

Now she was about to step into that and yet something seemed to hold her back. Hold her here, in Wayne's arms. It felt so good, it was so safe. He gave her everything she had never had with Hutch.

But that was just sentimental. A bunch of feelings that were like this night: a special occasion, a onetime occurrence. She need not act on it, need not disturb everything she had just secured. She had to be strong now.

Wayne himself had said it was okay for her to leave. He might feel attracted to her but he wasn't about to commit to her. He was a loner who liked to do things his way. A man who lived for his horses and dogs, his land and his cattle. He didn't need a girlfriend to distract him, let alone a wife who would share his home and make demands on him.

She pulled back and said, breathlessly, "Thanks for everything you did for me. It means a lot."

Wayne looked into her eyes. "I'm glad it helped." His voice was low, vibrating inside of her. He didn't say more but just leaned in. Erin didn't move. She wanted him to do this. She wanted one more kiss. It couldn't hurt. She wasn't being dishonest. He knew she was leaving. That she had to leave. That whatever seemed to connect them couldn't stand the test of time. They had to leave it be.

They had to…

His lips brushed hers and she just sank into the feeling. She didn't want to think anymore, to try to reason about it. She wanted to feel that he was there for her, that she was here for him. That they somehow seemed to be made for each other.

Over their heads fireworks exploded and colored the skies red, green and blue. But they didn't notice. They were lost in each other.

CHAPTER SEVENTEEN

MATT CARPENTER STOOD looking up at the sky full of colors, drinking in the beauty of the display without really feeling it inside. There was something restless about him all day long, and he couldn't shake it, not even now as the festivities wound down and night fell over their little town.

"Hey handsome," April moved closer against him. "What are you thinking about?"

He sheltered her in his arms, realizing how fortunate he was to have her here. To rest his chin on her shoulder and close his eyes for a moment.

April brushed her hand through his hair. "You were quiet," she observed. "What is the matter? You can tell me." He heard a touch of worry in her voice. Maybe she was thinking he was hiding something from her. Something he didn't want her to know.

And he was. But it wasn't something major. Not like she might suspect.

He sighed. "You always see right through me."

"That is what wives are for." She rested her warm hand in his neck. "Now out with it, Mr. Carpenter."

Matt said at her ear, "Are you sorry you gave up cruising?"

It was silent. He felt like it was too silent almost. Of course it wasn't really silent as there were still fireworks exploding above them and people were cheering and talking but she was silent.

He lifted his head to look at her. See the truth in her face. "You are, aren't you?" he said, pain gnawing at his heart. "I knew the moment I heard you talking with Erin. You told her about the things you had given up to be able to live here with me and..."

"You listened in on our conversation?" April asked softly. Her eyes were wide and questioning, but not accusing. "Why, Matt? I have no secrets from you."

"I came to the door and I overheard by accident. Then I lingered on purpose to hear more. I was just worried that...you're not happy here.

That you do love me but that the small-town life is…a bit boring for you."

April laughed softly. "I guess it is true what they say that when you listen in on conversations that are not meant for you to hear you often hear unwelcome things."

Matt pressed his heels into the ground. "So it is true. You do miss it."

"Sometimes I remember waking up in the port of an exciting metropolis waiting to be explored and I do miss the excitement of it and the unknown beckoning to be discovered. But I never wish I was still there. Because I want to be here. With you." She said it with conviction. "I can't help that I saw a lot of the world and that sometimes I wonder what the cherry blossom season looks like in Tokyo each spring, or that I wish I could see another koala and baby in the Australian bush. But I never feel like I sacrificed those things to be here. On the contrary. I feel very lucky. Because those were wonderful experiences, but they were moments in time. Here I have a lifetime of happiness. With you."

Matt's heart grew light. He wished he had discussed this sooner and not carried the load alone, feeling more somber about it as days went by. It had not been necessary. April was his and would stay his. Somehow he made her happy and she wanted to be with him. Which was a great and undeserved gift.

April stood on tiptoe to brush a kiss on his lips. “Next time you hear me say something, you just ask what I mean. Don’t go grouching about it.”

“I never grouch.”

“No?” She laughed but her eyes were serious when she continued, “My life is here now, Matt, and I couldn’t be happier about it. The ranch hotel, the horses, making sure the guests have a good time, it all feels like I belong there. It has been like that ever since I came to work for you when Belle was still little. Sometimes I can’t believe she is all grown up now and vacationing in Canada with her college friends. It seems only a short while ago that I held her in my arms or pushed her on the swing. Those memories mean so much to me. They showed me that…there may be a hundred places in the world where you can feel happy but there is only one place where you belong. Where you are truly at home. For me that is with you.”

He wrapped his arms around her and held her close. “And for me that is with you. I love you, April.”

“I love you too.” She leaned against him and

let out a sigh of happiness. Then she said softly, "I hope Erin will find a love like we have. She deserves it. Her two-timing fiancé may have turned her against the idea of ever marrying but… I think she should really have someone to tell her how special she is. It does wonders for one's self-confidence." She fell silent a moment and added, "I don't think she realizes that Wayne really likes her."

Matt's eyes widened involuntarily. "Wayne?" he queried. "Isn't he just the lone cowboy who rides into the sunset? I never saw a family man in him."

"Maybe not but… There is something when they are together. I can't explain it. Maybe I just want to see it because a connection to town would mean Erin will be back here. I guess I realized over the past few days what a great friend she makes." April smiled up at him. "I may be a little prejudiced about wanting to keep people here in Heartmont. Because this town feels like home."

CHAPTER EIGHTEEN

WAYNE DRAGGED HIMSELF from the house to the stables. It really was the morning after. The big festivities had carried on deep into the night and it had been two o'clock before his head had hit the pillow. His alarm clock had cruelly interrupted his beautiful dream of walking in the mountains with Erin. They had held hands and laughed and enjoyed the scenery. Everything inside him had been perfectly at peace. He had never felt so happy in his entire life. But then…beep beep beep. He had tried to will the annoying sound away and linger in his dreamland but it wasn't meant to be. The drowsiness had faded and he had woken up to reality. The reality that he had to feed his animals and dive into a new day full of hard work. And the reality that on this very day Erin was leaving town. She wasn't walking in the mountains with him, hand in hand. Far from it. They had decided they couldn't be together and she was leaving.

The weight of the whole situation had hit him like a ton of bricks. Now as he walked to the stables, he felt every muscle in his body ache as if some wild horse had thrown him and he had hit the ground hard.

It was true that losing Erin felt like the biggest setback he had ever experienced. He had been through a lot over time but this was... Maybe it was because he had opened up to someone, shared feelings when he had believed he never could. He had suddenly, maybe just a little, believed he could be relationship material after all. That he need not be that eternal bachelor. But now the dream was over. The dream he had this night and the dream he had built in his mind as he got to know Erin. She had never intended to stay here. She had only been stranded, against her will. Heartmont had been but a detour in her life.

He had to convince himself that she would not have any regrets about leaving the town, or him, or he might get stupid things into his head like driving out to the ranch hotel and asking her to stay.

Begging her to stay maybe? It already felt empty without her.

He went inside the stables and stood a moment attuning himself to the peace and quiet in there. The animals were still drowsy and there was a calm in the air that was healing. He had often come here to soak it up into his very being. Because he felt it, he believed it could also heal the scared and nervous horses he took in. But for some it was a lot harder than for others.

He looked at the box that held the frightened mare. He so wished he could do more for her. But it took time. He had to trust in the process. He knew that with his mind, but his heart didn't want to agree. It wanted to heal the pain *now.* It wanted to save her *now.*

He gently started talking to her. The moment she heard his voice her ears perked forward and she looked in his direction. There was a moment of interest, of connection, before the fear kicked in and her ears went flat. She stepped back, as if to avoid his nearness even as he stayed away from her box. "It's okay, girl," he said softly, "it's okay. I won't hurt you. If only you understood..."

She watched him with suspicion, the white of her eyes showing. He knew she wasn't ready to be approached more directly and with a sigh he went to get her food and water. Even if he came bearing those gifts, she distrusted him. It would be a long road to take her to a better place. But he would keep trying. That was what he did.

He put her food and water in her stall and stepped back to see what she did. She looked at him again and her ears were moving forward. She reached out her muzzle tentatively, not to take a bite of her breakfast but to breathe his scent it seemed. She held her head out to him like that, her body tense but still…

He held his breath as he reached out his hand. If he misread her now, she might snatch at him and injure him. He had to make sure that he was faster than she was, if things went wrong.

But she wasn't panicking yet. She stood very still, waiting for his fingers to close the distance and touch her gingerly. There was this moment where he could give her the briefest brush across the side of her muzzle. Then she stepped back and he withdrew his hand. But she was calmer than other mornings, and when he retreated a few more paces, she started drinking which she normally avoided when he was close. She seemed to be lowering her defenses. Slowly. But surely.

Joy raced through him and he wished he could share this with someone. That he could go outside and find Erin there. That they could have breakfast together.

But she wasn't here. He was all alone. And he would stay that way. Because she was packing to leave.

When he came from the stables, to go back to the house and have his lone breakfast, the sun shone exactly on the rosebush from which he had given some roses to Erin for the display at the community center. Their special color seemed to light up as if the flowers themselves produced light. He had seen it before in early morning, but this time it seemed more pronounced and special. It was like they were beaming at him, reminding him of the power of love. His grandparents had had a wonderful marriage. They had loved and supported each other for sixty years. Even if he hadn't spent much time with them after his mother had died, he knew what their bond had been made of. It was as though the roses were telling him that right now.

He couldn't just walk past them and go inside and make porridge. No. He stopped and looked them over with a wistful smile. "She's leaving town today," he said. "It is probably for the best, huh? Her parents want her back, she can have a great career with them. They do love her, her sister does too. Erin needs to be cared for and protected by people who will support her. Who will be there for her. I should be glad for her. I told her I was, you know."

He went back over their conversation. He had done what he believed was right in letting her go. There was no point in telling her he needed her here. What could he offer her? He would be like Hutch, who had drawn her into some fake fantasy about a life together while everything he offered was quicksand. Had been built on lies and deception.

The breeze moved the flowers and it seemed like they were slowly shaking. Shaking their little heads at his analysis? That he was anything like Hutch?

Hutch had been a con man, a liar and cheat. He had never loved Erin but wanted to use her for his own purposes. He had wanted the money she could bring in but never her. Did Wayne want money from Erin? Of course not. Did he want to use her to get anything or move forward in life? No, absolutely not. So why would he be like Hutch?

Why would he feel like he had nothing to offer her? He did have a home here. A pretty nice ranch. With animals which she loved. She had adored the puppies and shown a real interest in the frightened mare. She had also felt right at home in their small-town community working with people for the anniversary celebrations. She already had a friend in April and had connected with her extended family. If Erin wanted to give him a chance, she would already have connections here. Why would he believe she had no future here?

Because I am afraid, he answered his own question. *I am afraid of asking her to commit to me and then finding she is not happy here. I want...reassurances, certainties.*

But life doesn't work that way. You have to take chances on the things you believe in.

He suddenly saw, sharply, that he had always done that. That anything that had been worthwhile in his life had demanded taking a chance, taking risk. Buying this land, building his house, accepting animals who only cost him money and time. Getting into committees, standing in for Cade… It was always about doing what he knew was right without counting the costs or avoiding the risks attached. That was how he lived. He had done it when no one had supported him. When his father had been disappointed and Alex had warned him it would never work out. But he had done it anyway, because he had felt he had to do what he believed in.

It might still hurt that Dad and Alex had never come to understand his choices. It was best when family supported the dreams one had. But it wasn't necessary. Life could also be good without their approval. If he kept waiting for that, he could wait for the rest of his life. He had to believe in his own choices regardless. And deep down inside he knew that he always had. His ranch had become what it was today because of conviction. Beliefs that he had to do this and that it would make him happy.

And now this wonderful woman had stepped into his life, had run into it in her wedding dress asking for a lift into town, and he was hinking about letting her go? She had fallen straight into his arms at the resort, and instead of grabbing her and holding onto her, he was thinking of releasing her back into the world she had run from?

He did believe it was good for her to make up with her parents and restore family relations, if possible. But did he really think she had to work in their business to be happy? To feel that she was somebody? No. She was already amazing. She had achieved success on her own.

Why had he not told her that? Why had he said all the things that seemed appropriate but also felt like an easy cop-out? Not acknowledging how he felt? How she felt?

She had responded to his kiss. She was falling for him too. But he had not wanted to address that. Because it was complicated? Or because she had come too close? Wasn't he acting like that horse in his stable? Hiding behind fear and pain as an excuse not to open up and take a risk?

But this morning the mare had given him a chance. For the first time she had shown she wanted to let him in. That she might not be able to conquer all the past trauma at once, but that they could get there, step by step. If they were only willing to try.

He moved closer to the bush with roses. They seemed to invite him over with their luminous petals. He reached out and selected the most beautiful one. He took it in his palm and looked it over with a smile before gently removing it from the bush. "You are going to do something very special for me," he said softly. "You are going to be an invitation. An invitation not for a date or for an afternoon together. No. For a lifetime."

The cold morning air made him shiver. Or

was it nerves that crept across his spine and settled in his stomach as he realized what he was about to do? How he was about to upset everything that had seemed settled and dealt with last night?

Did he really want to take these chances? Did he want to ask her to be with him when she had already packed her suitcase to leave? Her parents expected her to leave. Her sister was happy things had turned out this way. What would he be doing to Erin by presenting her with this choice?

Still… She had to know there was a choice. That she didn't have to go with her parents because she had no alternative. She did have one. Right here.

He took a deep breath and then headed for his truck. He had to do this. No matter what happened next.

ERIN LOOKED INTO the mirror, seeing the concern in her eyes. Morning had broken with the realization she was going home with her parents. Part of her was very glad and relieved that they weren't angry with her and even wanted her back in the firm. It was more than she had hoped for. But at the same time it felt like…she was leaving unfinished business here. Wayne and she…

Erin rubbed her face. It wasn't possible. She could not be falling for him so soon after she had believed herself to be in love with Hutch and was about to marry him.

But her relationship with Hutch had been under pressure for some time. The way in which he had taken over plans for the wedding. The uneasiness she felt around his family and friends. She had never truly fitted in. She had felt like a stranger, an outsider. She had never fully surrendered herself to Hutch, even though she had agreed to become his wife.

After running away from the resort and the wedding ceremony she had felt humiliated and disappointed but also strangely free. Free to have escaped a permanent bond with a man she had not fully trusted.

It had been so different with Wayne. She had never pretended with him. Never had to fake being somebody she wasn't. He had known her situation and still he had not judged. He hadn't considered her a failure. On the contrary, he had built her up and helped her.

He had also needed her. She had been able to reach out and touch him and help him with issues of his own. He had shown her vulnerability where Hutch had been about bravado and show. With Wayne she had shared more personal stuff in the short while they had known each other than in the months with Hutch. Now she was moving back into the life that had always been waiting for her and it seemed almost like…she was doing the wrong thing. Like she was running away again, this time because she was afraid of what she could have right here if she was only brave enough to stay.

Erin pulled her hands away from her face and looked at her mirror image. "You are not chickening out," she said more loudly than she intended.

Hurriedly she continued, softer, "You are going back home with Mom and Dad and Livia and you are going to work in the firm and be a success. For them but also for yourself. To prove to yourself you can do it. That you are better than you ever believed. That is what you need. Reassurance after the blows dealt to your ego by the wedding fiasco. You need to build things up, not cause new chaos by suddenly deciding you don't want to leave. Why stay anyway? Wayne never said he wanted you to. He even encouraged you to leave."

Yes, his words had said that. His kiss had said something else.

But it had only been a kiss. Not a confession of love, not an offer to give them a try. Just a kiss.

A goodbye kiss.

Erin sighed and turned away from the mirror. She wished she could just embrace this day and the joy of reuniting with her parents without feeling so torn about it all. Without thinking of Wayne and missing him already. If later today she drove away from Heartmont, would not a piece of her heart stay here with him?

There was a knock on the door of her room. That would probably be breakfast. It was delivered in a basket with hot toast, fresh juice and all kinds of other delicious goodies. She didn't feel like eating much but she had to have something to start the day well. Mom and Dad would be coming soon.

She opened the door and leaned down to pick up the basket. Then her hand stalled midair. In the basket, resting on the checkered tea towel that covered the food, was a single rose from Wayne's bush. It lay there like a sign, a secret message. *Hello, remember me?*

She touched the tender petals with a fingertip. This bush was unique. April and Matt didn't have one like it. This rose wasn't included with the breakfast they served. It had been added.

Wayne!

Was he here? Was he…

She felt her heartbeat speed up. She picked up the rose and holding it in her hand, headed quickly out to the yard.

CHAPTER NINETEEN

SHE HEARD THE sound of an engine indicating someone was pulling away. She pushed herself to hurry but once outside she couldn't see a truck. If Wayne had been here, he was gone already. He had left her the rose and vanished.

Was it a goodbye rose? Was it one last gesture to end this beautiful time they'd had together? Could she just save it and dry it and look at it sometimes to remind her of a very special friend who had helped her in a time of need?

No. Everything inside of her resisted this conclusion. She didn't want to consider this goodbye. She wanted to consider it like…

She held her breath. She felt the stem of the rose between her fingertips, the warmth of the sunshine on her face, she heard birdsong. It all etched itself into her brain as she stood there and let the truth sink in. She was falling in love with Wayne and she didn't want to say goodbye to him. She didn't want to leave town and go work with her parents. She wanted to stay right here and get to know Wayne much better. She wanted to spend a lot more time with him, sitting over pancakes, having picnics, exploring the Rockies, tending to his horses, helping him find owners for the puppies. She wanted to be a part of his life here. She wanted to be with him and see him smile, watch the expressions on his face as he was concentrating on something or suddenly had to laugh. She wanted to see that quiver of pain when the death of his mother came up so she could put her hand on his arm and make him feel better. She wanted to be there for him, knowing he would be there for her. That it had been like that between them from the start. Right after they had met. She didn't understand it. There was no logic to it. But it was real.

As real as the ground she stood on and the scent of horses on the air. As real as the morning breeze caressing her face. As real as everything she had done here. Here in Heartmont she had learned how to live. How to open up, how to believe in herself and how to connect with others. This had been the most beautiful time of her life, despite the heartache that had started it all. She had lost something she had believed to be very important to her, only to find that it hadn't been important at all and she had never realized what truly mattered.

She could not go with Mom and Dad and step back in the rat race of impressing clients and going to parties and having to be perfect all the time. She didn't need food from delis or art museums or public transport at three in the morning. She didn't truly need any of the things she had loved about the city. What she did need was acceptance. Unconditional acceptance. She wanted to stay here where it was okay to run into the grocery store in dirty jeans because you had been busy with your livestock all day long and forgotten you needed milk for dinner. Everything here was down-to-earth and practical and self-evident in a very reassuring way. Best of all, she didn't need to change a thing about herself. She was okay the way she was.

She lifted the rose to her face and inhaled its delicate aroma. "Thanks Wayne," she whispered, "for being who you are. For being exactly what I needed."

"Erin!" April's voice resounded from behind and Erin spun to face her friend.

April said, "Have you spoken to Wayne? He caught me taking out breakfast to you and asked if he could do it. I figured he wanted to see you briefly before you leave later today." There was a quiet interest in her eyes, but she didn't ask any questions.

Erin hesitated a moment, then said, "I didn't see him. He left the breakfast basket outside my door. With this." She showed April the rose.

April held her gaze. "Is…something going on between the two of you?" She added in a rush, "You don't have to tell me, Erin, if it's private, but…just last night I mentioned to Matt how much I want you to be happy. And that you might be happy getting to know Wayne a lot better. See, Wayne is not a player like some people seem to think. They feel he takes life too easily and is never quite serious. But I've known him much longer, because he is Cade's best buddy, and I can tell you he is a great guy with a heart of gold. I so want to see him happy as well. If the two of you got together…"

Erin's heart grew warm under the passion in April's voice. It was so nice to see how people appreciated Wayne for who he was. Did he himself even know? Maybe not. But it was time that changed. She said, "I also want him to be happy. I just don't know if… I can be the one to make him happy, you know. I just landed in this town, I am a city girl, I…"

April reached out and put a hand on her arm. "Those are all reasons in your head, Erin. I had a million when I fell back in love with Matt. I was only here for a few weeks, I had been newly promoted to officer, I was about to embark on a grand adventure in my career. I didn't know if Matt cared for me at all, I wasn't sure about the past we shared and…how I felt about moving back to this town where everyone saw me as a little girl, a tomboy to mother. But my heart was telling me one thing loud and clear. That I was still connected to Matt. That I had never stopped loving him. That I had always compared every man I met to him. And they had never ever lived up. I knew I had to do something with the feeling. Explore it, take it seriously, give it a chance. Or I would be forever sorry that I hadn't."

She squeezed Erin's arm. "I can only tell you this. If you feel that there is something inside of you that reaches out to him, you have to find out where it can take you. You deserve that chance. And so does Wayne."

Erin nodded. The warmth that had lit up inside of her as April talked about Wayne being such a wonderful guy now filled her whole being. He did deserve that she stayed here for him. To explore the feelings between them. To give their bond the room to grow.

April said, "I don't want to make things hard for you now that you were all decided to go with your folks, but..."

As she spoke, a taxi entered the yard and the door opened. Mom came out smiling at Erin. "I'm so glad, darling, that we are going home together."

Erin felt a cold sensation skitter across her back. She had to tell them right away. "Mom, I... I can't come today. I have to stay here a little longer and think things through. It all happened so fast, there was no time to consider..." She took a deep breath. "I have been away for years, cruising, doing my own things. I'm just not sure I fit back into the firm. I know how much you want that, Dad and you, but... I have to consider what is right for me. Give me some time to think it over and come to a decision that is not spur-of-the-moment."

Mom stared at her. For a moment she seemed to want to argue and put pressure on her but then she released her breath in a huff. "Well, that is the thing with grown-up children. They have to forge their own path in life. Come to their own decisions. I guess if we bundle you into this taxi now and take you home, you will go away again. We did learn that when you went cruising. Your father told me a thousand times you'd be back but I knew better. We had pushed you too hard and it only had the reverse effect. It alienated you from us. I never want to go through that again. I was so glad when we met yesterday and could have lunch and catch up. Like families do. It's much better if you decide you want to come back into the firm of your own accord."

Erin looked at her father who had got out to stand beside the taxi, watching them with a frown over his eyes. She went over to him and kissed him on the cheek. "I'm so happy, Dad, that you came to see my floral work here and that we celebrated together. I can't tell you how much it means to me that…you are not upset about Hutch and me. I made mistakes there and…"

Her father shook his head. "We will not mention it again, Erin. It's in the past. We have forgiven you. You should also forgive yourself."

Erin felt like lightning had struck her. She should forgive herself? Was that not the whole problem? That she had not forgiven herself for the mistake she had made in trusting Hutch and allowing him to take over her entire life.

She still blamed herself for it and realized

she had taken Mom and Dad's offer to work off her guilt as it were. But it wasn't necessary. They had forgiven her and if she could only forgive herself, she was free to move on.

In whatever direction she chose.

She wrapped her arms around her father's neck and hugged him tightly. "Thanks, Dad, this means the world to me. To know you are not angry with me..."

His arms closed around her and he said, in a hoarse voice, "Little Erin... I could never stay angry with you long. You are my baby, always will be."

Erin released him with tears in her eyes. "You are the best." She also hugged her mother. "I will be in touch soon. We must call regularly."

Mom nodded. "Take care, Erin. And give Livia a call too, from time to time."

Erin swallowed hard. "Livia won't be happy to hear I didn't go with you."

"Call her anyway. She is still your big sister."

They got back into the taxi and left the yard. Erin looked after the vehicle with an intense sense of relief. She had done the right thing not going with them. This was about more than her professional future. About more than coming back into the company or not. It was about not doing what she always did. Make decisions to please others, to be someone they wanted her to be. It was about time she became the Erin she wanted to be. The woman she had always been deep inside but had been afraid to show to the outside world.

Wayne had seen that woman. And he had fallen for her. Now Erin wanted to be with him. She said to April, "I have to go to Wayne, can I borrow your car?"

"Sure. I'll get you the keys."

Erin stood there, holding the rose Wayne had gifted her. Her knees felt jittery and full of jelly. She was willing to go all in with Wayne, but was he commited to do the same? What if she had read him wrong? What if he had never meant for her to stay here? What if…

She lifted her face to the sky and forced herself to smile. *I'll find out about that soon. I am going to see him and tell him how I feel.*

CHAPTER TWENTY

WHEN ERIN DROVE into the yard of Wayne's ranch, she immediately noticed that his truck wasn't there. Disappointment shot through her. Wasn't he home? She got out of April's car and looked around. There didn't seem to be anybody inside the house. Finally at the back of the barn she found his ranch hand at work with Birch's daughter Frey by his side. The dog looked her over with a friendly interest as she approached. The ranch hand told her Wayne had gone out because there was a horse roaming on someone's land and it had to be caught. "He is a real horse whisperer," he said with a wink. "They always want him. You can try and give him a call if it's urgent. But he won't be picking up his phone, I suppose. Not when he's busy."

Erin nodded. "Is it okay for me to sit on the porch and wait for him?"

"Of course. I'm almost done with these

chores and then I'm going into town to get some lumber for repairs. But do make yourself at home."

Erin went to sit on the porch and looked about her, drinking in everything. She wondered if Wayne would be away long and if he would have a hard time catching the runaway horse. The ranch hand left in a small pickup truck. It was so quiet. She had never realized that the countryside was so peaceful. That it had a way of taking life down a few notches to a more pleasant pace. Earlier she had craved the buzz of the city to drown out the uneasy questions inside about what her life really meant and where she was headed. But now she saw it all clearly and the quiet didn't daunt her anymore. She felt right at ease with it.

She had pinned the rose to her dress and gave it a loving look as she sat there. It was back where it belonged now. At home where the rest of the bush was. But this one she would always keep, to remind herself of this special day.

Her phone rang and she picked up. It was Livia. The moment Erin realized, a little dread grabbed her. Livia might always be her big sister, like Mom had said, but that didn't mean they couldn't disagree.

"I heard you are not flying home with Mom and Dad," Livia said. Her voice was a little sharp. "How come? I thought it was all decided last night."

"Dad asked me to come back into the firm and I said that I might do that, not that I was going to jump right in. I do need time to get back on my feet after the way Hutch treated me."

Livia was silent a moment. Then she said, "I do need you to come back, Erin. I want to do more party planning and I can't as long as Mom and Dad lean on me so much."

So Livia had also wanted something for herself out of this reunion. It was understandable, but Erin didn't want to cater to other people's needs anymore. Not at the cost of her own happiness. "I realize, but I have my own life. I can't just upend everything."

"Why not? You quit cruising to marry Hutch. You are technically unemployed."

"Yes, and maybe I want to stay that way for a few weeks. Livia, there is no rush for me to commit to anything right now."

Livia was silent as if she couldn't quite grasp why anyone would want to stay unemployed when there was a great job up for grabs. Finally she said, "You need to save face. A cancelled wedding is a terrible humiliation. You have to take a step up to feel better about yourself."

Erin was sad Livia felt that way, but not long ago she herself had harbored comparable thoughts. Had believed that it was essential to always prove yourself. She felt almost sorry for her sister that she didn't understand what was truly important in life. "And getting back into the firm can give me that?"

"It's not a small thing. The firm is worth millions. If you become a full partner, you will have all the status to attract a good man."

Erin blinked. Was this really what Livia had imagined for her? "Wow. In a few words you offer me money, status, success and even a wealthy husband? How could I refuse?"

"Why so rebellious? I know you like freedom but you can't escape from your destiny. Mom and Dad worked hard to build an empire they want to hand down to us. As their daughters we do have a responsibility."

"I also have a responsibility toward myself. Toward my own dreams and wishes."

"You are not eight anymore blowing out your birthday candles and making wishes." Livia's voice grew sharper. "You have to accept your duties now."

"Then you cut down on the party planning

and accept *your* duties." Erin sat up straighter to win this struggle. "You don't want to be hemmed in by the business either. You also want more than just doing what Mom and Dad ask. Being who they dreamt you up to be. Now let me do the same."

Livia sighed. "You haven't changed at all. I thought the disaster with Hutch had taught you something."

"It did. It taught me that I have to stop being what other people want me to be. And become who I want to be."

There was a deep silence. Then Livia said, "Okay. I won't try to force you into anything. That won't work anyway. I just hope you know what you are doing. It's the rancher, right? I saw the way he looked at you. He must have told you some story about how he is in love with you and you can be together… But that's just silly. You have nothing in common with a man like that."

"How would you know? Did you even talk to him?"

"I didn't have to. I know how those people live."

"Really? You've never spent time in a small town."

"No, but I saw a documentary about it once.

The hardships of country life. Ranchers care for cows from dawn to dusk. They can never have a holiday abroad because they have to milk their cows. If there is bad weather, the entire crop is lost and they have to take an extra loan at the bank. I bet his house is triple mortgaged."

The way in which Livia desperately reached for reasons to deter her from falling for Wayne made Erin laugh. It was much too late for that. She sat here on the steps of this potentially triple-mortgaged house and all she could think was: *I hope Wayne manages to catch the horse safely and that he comes home and we can have pancakes together.*

Livia took a deep breath and said, "Really, Erin, do you have any idea what you are getting into? I only want to protect you from another disaster. You are vulnerable now." Her voice carried genuine concern. "You're not thinking this through."

"Maybe not. But I only know one thing. I feel differently than I have ever felt before. And I want to keep feeling this way."

Livia sighed. Irritation had clearly taken over. "You are truly impossible. From one man who was all wrong for you to the next. And all because of feelings. Feelings can't be trusted.

You have to make decisions with your brain. Use some common sense. You are not a teen anymore. Can't you just grow up?"

"Maybe you just have to stop treating me like you are my mother. You're my big sister but you are not responsible for my happiness. Nor to clean up after me if I make mistakes."

Livia scoffed. "Oh no? Isn't that just what I did? I made sure Mom and Dad didn't find out about the bill sent to the firm. I tried to set up a reconciliation. I even wanted you back with us in the company. I worked hard to make it all possible, setting aside my own feelings about the matter. And now you respond like this. I think it's really ungrateful on your part."

Earlier these words would have upset Erin and she would have felt small and dejected. But now she clearly saw the truth. And she knew she had to tell Livia this truth whether her sister wanted to hear it or not. "I'm sorry you feel that way. But we must both change our dynamics, or we will never have a good relationship. I have to stop pleasing you and you have to stop—"

"Pleasing me?" Livia cut her short. "Trust me, Erin, the last thing you are doing is pleasing me. If you were pleasing me, you'd now be with Mom and Dad flying home."

For a few moments there was silence as if Livia looked for something to say, anything that might still help her win the argument.

Erin realized that for once her sister had run out of persuasive tactics to offer. It was painful to realize Livia had also always done what she felt was expected of her. Maybe she was unhappy too but didn't know how to change the situation.

"I'm sorry to let you down," she said. "But you will find a way to keep party planning. I know you. You can make anything work."

"Thanks. I guess." Livia sounded resigned. "I tried my best to help you out. But if you want to do things differently… I just hope you won't be sorry later. Because despite of everything you might believe, I just want you to be secure. Take care. Bye." And with that she disconnected.

Erin stared at her phone. Yes, Livia no doubt meant it when she said she wanted her to be secure. But her ideas about security were far different from what Erin had discovered she needed. She couldn't make Livia understand. Livia would have to find out for herself, somehow, sometime. Discover that all the money and status in the world couldn't make her feel satisfied inside. That only acceptance and love could achieve that.

Erin sighed and put her phone away. She was going to wait for Wayne. No matter how long it took. She had made up her mind, she knew what she wanted. And no one was going to sway her now.

CHAPTER TWENTY-ONE

WAYNE DROVE BACK to his ranch with a head full of things he still had to do. Catching the horse had taken more time than he had figured, but they had finally calmed the animal enough to load him into a van and get him back to his owner. Before he left, the local who'd assisted Wayne had reminded him that they'd see each other tonight at the meeting. A meeting Wayne had forgotten all about but where he was supposed to present a slide show about water management. He rubbed his forehead a moment. He had to stop letting himself be talked into all of these things. But there was always a reason why he was the best man to do it. The others weren't familiar with the computer program, or they didn't have the time to prepare or... He guessed he should put his foot down more, but in a close-knit community it was hard to say no. Like you could never say no to family.

Erin hadn't been able to say no. He understood that. Her parents had been very gracious to invite her back into the company. It was a grand gesture on their part. It would be like his father asking him to take over the bookshop or something.

Wayne couldn't see himself doing that, though. His lifestyle was so different, it would just not be a match. And he honestly wondered if Erin fit into her parents' fast-paced lifestyle.

But she had to try, he supposed. The things you did because your family asked you to…

He turned into the road leading to his ranch. His shoulders ached from the exertion of controlling the horse. He hadn't eaten much and lack of coffee was burning a hole in his brain. But the main thing was Erin. It was so strange to know she wasn't in town anymore. That he couldn't call her and see her. That she was far away and she would not be back either.

The rose hadn't made a difference. Maybe he should have known. That life wasn't like it was presented in the movies. That a romantic gesture couldn't suddenly solve everything. Bridge the gap between them. He was a country guy, she was a city girl. She had recently had her heart broken too. How could he expect her to fall for him so quickly?

He caught sight of his house and the first

thing he noticed was someone sitting on the porch steps waiting for him. He had turned off his phone during the rescue so the sounds wouldn't spook the horse and he had forgotten to turn it back on. Maybe there was something up in town and they needed his advice? As long as he could have coffee first.

But when he closed in, he realized that it was a woman and he knew her well. *Erin...*

Erin was on the ranch, waiting for him. She had not left with her parents. She wasn't on her way back to her high-society lifestyle. She was still here. Here!

He parked the truck and jumped out, rushed to meet her. She came to her feet and beamed at him. Her hand touched the rose that she had pinned to her dress. "Thanks for this."

He stared at her, drinking in her beautiful face, her lovely eyes and wonderful smile. He said, "You, uh, had to wait a long time to say that. I mean, if I had known you were here, I wouldn't have stayed away so long."

"I thought you had a horse to catch?"

"I did but..."

"It wouldn't let itself be caught sooner even if it knew I was here." Her eyes sparkled with amusement. "And I know you are too responsible to leave early. You wanted to do a good job and save the horse."

"It's safe now. Back with its owner. It got away when the bridle broke. It isn't a difficult animal like my charges."

"Good." She nodded at him, then gestured at the house. "I didn't want to go inside and rifle through your things, but now that you are here, I could make us coffee."

"Yes, please. I haven't had a single cup today and I am just..."

"Decaffeinated." She pulled a serious expression. "We must remedy that."

In a few minutes he was sitting at his kitchen table watching her make coffee and bake eggs. It was like she had always been there. Like she belonged here. It was odd because he knew that she was bound for the city and her old life, but he didn't care right now. He wanted to live these moments to replay them in his mind later. Later when she would be gone.

"There." Erin put a plate in front of him with buttered toast and eggs. "You need to eat something. How can you work when you don't eat?"

"I just had to go after this call and..." He gestured.

She said sternly, "Shut up and eat."

While he ate, she was pouring him coffee

and tidying up at the sink. It was nice to have someone around who could do things for him. That he didn't have to do this himself. That he could just sit and enjoy this.

Finally he asked, "Why are you still here? I mean, I expected you to leave today with your folks."

"Oh, they did leave. They understood I needed some more time, that everything had happened so fast and… They were okay with it. Livia's not. She called me to tell me I was being irresponsible and childish and whatnot. She will always go into big sister mode like that."

"How did you feel?" he asked with a worried frown.

Erin shrugged. "I guess I did cringe a little but… I have to learn not to jump through every hoop Livia holds up for me. I have to forge my own path. Livia had her own hidden agenda all along. She wants to do more party planning and needs me to work with Mom and Dad to free up her time. But she'll have to fight for that on her own. Knowing her she can do it."

Wayne nodded. Now that he had eaten he felt better. Nice and almost drowsy. He settled back in his chair. "If you do go back later and work with her, you have to ensure you know how to tell her no, or she will be calling all the shots."

Erin sat down opposite him. She also had a mug of coffee. “I know. I started wondering if it is smart to go and work with them at all. It brings up too many memories of how things always were. I am not that person anymore. I don’t want to be.” She blew in her coffee.

Wayne watched her expression. He wanted to know more but waited for her to continue.

Erin said, “I feel like the whole thing with Hutch taught me one thing. I can’t be what someone else wants me to be. I can’t fake it or playact all the time. I have to be me.”

“Which is more than enough, I tell you.”

She looked up at him. “Do you really think so?”

“Of course. I never wanted to change anything about you.”

ERIN STARED IN Wayne’s honest eyes. She knew he wasn’t making this up to make her feel better. He meant it. He meant everything he said. She could count on him.

“That is why I am here,” she said. She put down the mug and reached for his hand. “Because you don’t want to change me. I want to be with someone who takes me for me. No questions asked.”

Wayne smiled at her. It softened the tight

lines in his face. "I am glad you are here. I missed you when I drove back. I mean, I wondered where you were now and…"

Erin gestured to the rose with her free hand. "You left me this."

"Yes. I wanted you to know that…" He took a deep breath. "Maybe I went too fast saying it was okay for you to leave. That it was…" He faltered.

She squeezed his hand. "It's okay if you think this is kind of hard. I thought it was hard."

He eyed her. "What do you mean?"

"Admitting you need someone?" She said it softly. "Admitting that you are not immune to what another person thinks or says, and that you can get hurt."

Wayne's hand tightened at the word *hurt*. She gave him an encouraging sueeze. "I know your father never gave you a chance to be you. To become the person you wanted to be. But he was wrong wanting to change you. You are great. I don't think you could be any better. You're all I needed. I didn't see it at the time but…running away from my own wedding was the best thing that ever happened to me. It brought me to you."

A hesitant smile appeared on Wayne's face.

He turned over his hand and caught hers in it. He gently brushed his thumb over the back of her hand. "I guess at first I just wanted to save you. Like I save all kinds of things. Dogs, horses, committee meetings. I just can't help it. Let me do it. I have nothing better to do, you know." He clenched his jaw a moment. "It took me a while to realize I also needed you to save me. To show me that… I was hiding away from the world behind all the helpfulness and being this nice guy who always has a joke ready. I just didn't know how…"

Erin's expression was tender as she watched him. She didn't finish his sentence for him or said she understood. She just sat with him. Not trying to label his emotions or brush them aside saying it was okay.

Wayne said at last, "Grief changed me. Just because it wasn't allowed to exist. It became a part of me that I had to hide and I became good at hiding it. Until you came. With you I could talk about my mother and…it suddenly seemed easier. You never suggested I should be over it already."

Erin shook her head. "How could I ever do that? Missing her will stay a part of your life. But that is okay. It is okay, Wayne." She added after a short silence, "You are okay. Just let that sink in."

They sat and looked at each other holding each other's hand. They were okay. The way they were. With their mistakes and with the pain of the past. It didn't have to be changed or swept under the carpet. It was allowed to exist. And still they could be okay and have each other and be glad for that. Feel happiness shine on them like sunshine through the rain.

Erin said, "I'll pour you more coffee." She got up and went to the sink. Wayne rose too and came to stand behind her. He wrapped his arms around her waist. "You being here is the best thing that ever happened to me."

Erin smiled. "There is no place I would rather be."

EPILOGUE

"JUST A TOUCH to the left. That's it!" Erin stood back and sighed in satisfaction. The last of her floral decorations had just been attached to the rafters of the big barn on the ranch where Cody Brookes and Jackie Evans were marrying that afternoon. It was his folks' place, where he and Jackie were also going to live, in their own part of the large ranch house. Cody was a friend of Wayne's and via him Erin had gotten the assignment to do the flowers for the grand wedding feast later that day. The couple had wanted lots of sunflowers to brighten the day and it had worked out beautifully with the long tables where the guests and the bridal party would sit and the platform for the musicians and speeches. Erin was really looking forward to being a part of the festivities.

Weddings might have stayed a sore spot for her after the debacle with Hutch but she could honestly say she felt no pain at this moment.

On the contrary she felt gratitude and joy. She had found her community, the people she belonged with and most of all, the man who made her heart sing. Wayne was everything to her. He made her laugh, he listened to her stories, he encouraged her to dream big. Because of him, she was flying to Italy next week to take part in a floral decoration contest at a medieval castle. And Wayne had even offered to arrange for more help at the ranch and come with her so they could have some time off together. Who said that ranchers never had a holiday?

She so appreciated that he wanted to be part of what she loved. Even if the airplane ticket cost him money he needed for the ranch. He just took some extra handyman jobs around town to pay for the expenses. He was truly fantastic.

She remembered she still had a few more sunflowers left in the back of her car and went to get them to work them into the entry gate to the ranch. It would give a nice final touch to all the arrangements. Besides, the flowers should not go to waste but fulfill their purpose: making people happy on this big day.

As she leaned in to get the sunflowers, someone snuck up from behind. She caught the whiff of Wayne's aftershave before he locked her in his arms and kissed her. She kissed him back and melted into his embrace. The tension of wanting to get the floral arrangements all right was gone at once. He was with her and she felt so good.

Wayne said, "How are we with the last preparations? Anything I can do to help? I was with Cody a minute ago, but he is so nervous I can't stand to be around him. It makes my own brain melt down."

Erin laughed. "Poor you. Or rather poor Cody. I bet he didn't think he would ever feel nervous. He is always so down-to-earth."

"He just wants everything to be perfect for Jackie." Wayne shrugged. "Don't tell me I will one day be like that."

"I don't know." She held his gaze with a teasing look. "Maybe you don't even want a big wedding. Maybe we'll just tie the knot with the horses and the dogs present."

"Would you mind?" Wayne asked. "I bet once upon a time you wanted a fairy-tale wedding at a beautiful venue with all frills and bows attached."

"I guess I did." She remembered how worried she had been on the day she was to marry Hutch that her childhood dreams of the big wedding had not come true. How it had really bothered her. Now standing here with Wayne she could honestly say she just wanted to marry him, not really caring about the how and where. Having organized a wedding once she knew how expensive it could be. The expert intervention of Wayne's lawyer friend had ensured that Hutch had at least agreed to pay part of the bills. But still she had decided then and there that weddings need not cost that much to be memorable. The most important thing was the person she married. The man she could love and trust and be safe with.

Wayne let go of her and felt inside his pocket. He said softly, "I just picked it up. I wanted to save it for Italy. But why wait?" He sank down on bended knee and held the box out to her. Inside sparkled a ring with a heartshaped ruby. She stared at it. It was so gorgeous in the sunlight.

Wayne said softly, "Erin, darling… You know you are everything to me. Just stay with me always. Marry me."

"Yes, of course, Wayne, yes." She jumped at him and they fell over and tumbled onto the grass beside the car. Wayne laughed so hard tears formed in his eyes. "That was not very dignified."

"I don't care. I am just so so happy."

"Really?" he asked, his eyes full of tenderness.

"Yes. I am so happy because I found you. I love you."

"And I love you. More than I can ever say."

She lay there locked in his arms with the sun shining down on them and the scents of the land all around. The land that provided and sheltered and was their home. Her home too, now that she had settled here. It filled all of her senses until there was nothing but the joy of this moment.

Running away from a wedding that wasn't right for her she had run headfirst into the love of her life. It was almost unbelievable. But that was what all miracles were.

* * * * *